The
SECRET
ROOM

by NIKI YEKTAI

ORCHARD BOOKS • NEW YORK

Orchard Books, 95 Madison Avenue, New York, NY 10016

Manufactured in the United States of America
Book design by Mina Greenstein
The text of this book is set in 12 point Imprint.
2   4   6   8   10   9   7   5   3   1

Library of Congress Cataloging-in-Publication Data
Yektai, Niki.
The secret room / by Niki Yektai.   p.   cm.
Summary: When their family moves from a farm near
Albany to New York City in 1903, Katharine and her brother
must find ways to adjust to life in proper society.
ISBN 0-531-05456-X.   ISBN 0-531-08606-2 (lib. bdg.)
[1. Family life—Fiction. 2. City and town life—
Fiction. 3. New York (N.Y.)—Fiction.] I. Title.
PZ7.Y376Se   1992   [Fic]—dc20   92-6720

For Darius George Yektai

THE SECRET ROOM

·1·

KATHARINE OUTWATER held her mother's arm as they walked through the crowded streets of New York City. Mother was pushing baby Oswald in his carriage, while Katharine's brother Freddie took the lead. Freddie considered himself much older than Katharine, and he certainly looked it, being a good head taller; but in fact he was ten—just a year older.

"Now, Freddie, wait!" called Mother. "We're crossing the avenue together!" Freddie stopped while a couple of delivery wagons rattled by.

"Wait, Freddie!" she cried again. "Look at that reckless driver." A fancy victoria carriage raced past them.

"It's safe now," said Freddie. "I know how to cross the street."

"That's what you think, but you *don't,*" said Mother. "We're all new to New York, and if we're not careful, we'll end up under the wheels of a carriage or the hooves of a horse."

I

They crossed Madison Avenue and walked uptown toward their house. It was a gray day. Even on a sunny day, Katharine thought, New York City was all gray and brown—the buildings, the sidewalks, the streets. Only a few trees were growing out of holes in the pavement. Their leaves were a fresh green because it was late spring.

Mother had given Katharine a diary when they moved to New York, to record all her new and exciting experiences. Katharine had written that morning, *May 29, 1903. We have been in New York three weeks, and I still hate it.* Since Katharine was not fond of writing, she had added only the following:

> *I hate the crowds.*
> *I hate the noise.*
> *I hate the smell.*
> *I hate Uncle Harry's house.*
> *I hate Uncle Harry.*

This last was unfair, since she had never met Uncle Harry. He was Father's uncle, and he had died and left all his money and his house in New York to Father. The next thing Katharine knew, the farmhouse in the country outside Albany had been sold, and they had boarded a train and come to New York. Now they lived in Uncle Harry's gloomy brownstone house, which was partly covered with dark vines. It had four floors and a wooden attic with steep, slanting roofs, and was full of servants. In the rear there was a garden that Father said was large for the city. But it was tiny to a country girl, used to hayfields and forests. Katharine could cross the garden in four great leaps.

Only now that it was over and gone forever did Katharine realize what a happy life they had had in the country. She and Freddie had lessons with a tutor. But mostly they "ran wild," as their relatives in Albany said, playing with Clem and Clyde, the twin boys of their housekeeper. Father took the train into the city of Albany to practice law and returned in the evening. And Mother led a very quiet life, also caring for her dear papa, who was old and weak. It was his farm-house, and Mother had wanted to live with him during his last days. Those "last days" had happily gone on for many years. But not long after Grandpapa died, Uncle Harry died and left everything to Father. Katharine wished he had left it all to somebody else.

On the long train trip to New York, Mother had said, "Today we start a great adventure! Father is going to become a famous New York lawyer." But she never warned Katharine that she was going to change. Suddenly Mother was too busy to spend time with Katharine and her brothers. She left them with maids while she went out to pay calls on her new friends or to shop for furniture and clothes. Mother seemed to put on different clothes every hour.

Today, however, Katharine was happy: Mother had played with them all morning and taken them to a restaurant for lunch. Katharine hugged Mother's arm in both of hers as they walked up the avenue. As they

3

passed an empty lot, Freddie stopped by a pile of litter and pointed to a small wooden door on top.

"Oh, Mother, that's just what I need!" he exclaimed. "I haven't been able to do any carpentry because I haven't had a worktable. I can make one with this old door."

"Do you mean to carry it through the streets?" asked Mother.

Freddie nodded. "Please, Mother. You know how dull it's been without my carpentry."

Mother did not like to hear how dull it had been. She wanted everyone to love New York.

"Well, it is thrown in the garbage heap, so I suppose you can have it," she said. Freddie dragged the door behind him while passersby stared. *Bang, bang, thump.*

"I'll help you carry it," said Katharine eagerly. She lifted one end of the door despite Freddie's protests.

The door was heavy. Fortunately they were only two blocks from Uncle Harry's house, which was just off Madison on Seventy-third Street. Katharine helped Freddie carry the door up the front steps. The butler, Mr. Sloat, opened the door. He was English and had worked for Uncle Harry. Although short and gray and thin, he managed to look down his nose on everything. He was astonished by the old door, but before he could disapprove of its going through the marble hall and up the curved marble staircase, Katharine and Freddie had done it. They paused for breath on the second floor, then went past Father's library and the stately drawing room and up the red-carpeted stairs to the third floor. At one end were Father's and Mother's

4

rooms, and at the other end the nursery and the children's rooms.

Katharine and Freddie took the old door, which felt like a wagonload of bricks by now, into the nursery.

"All right, you can let go," said Freddie. "I could have managed alone." Katharine let it slam to the floor. She was mad. Freddie was leaving her out, as usual. He was always in a bad mood since their arrival in New York.

Mother came in, carrying Oswald. "Oh, Katharine, don't look so upset. You're going to do something with me," she said. She ran down the long hall to her rooms and returned with a large block of clay partly wrapped in a damp cloth. Soon Katharine and Mother were seated at the round nursery table, pounding clay, while Oswald ran happily around the room.

"I'm going to make something to brighten up this bare nursery," said Mother. "A vase." She laughed, and Katharine laughed with her. Mother had lit a fire in the fireplace. It made the nursery feel warm and cozy and reminded Katharine of their farmhouse, where the kitchen fire was always burning.

Katharine watched Mother make the vase. Mother was so pretty; everyone thought so. She was round and soft, with rosy cheeks and a tiny waist and silky blond hair piled high on her head. Katharine was just the opposite—all bones and angles, with a thin pale face and frizzy pale hair that she never combed if she could help it.

Katharine did not care about looking pretty. She cared much more about keeping up with Freddie, which was hard to do dressed in petticoats and ribbons. Recently she had been introduced to many of Father and Mother's new acquaintances. They called Freddie very handsome and "just like his father" with his straight sandy hair and ruddy cheeks and square shoulders. They thought two-year-old Oswald was darling. Then there was Katharine. No one admired her. Katharine decided that Freddie was Father's favorite because he was a boy and named after him. Oswald was Mother's favorite because he was the baby, so that left Katharine nobody's favorite. This had never entered her mind in the country. It was only in New York that she had begun to have such gloomy thoughts.

Katharine tried making a vase, but before long she got up to see what Freddie was doing. He had placed the door over two trunks; he had screwed on his vise and was sawing some old pieces of wood. His worktable didn't even shake.

"What are you making?" asked Katharine.

"Shelves for the nursery. Mother, tell Katharine to leave me alone."

"What makes you think I want to help make those ugly old shelves?" said Katharine. She sat down.

The sides of Katharine's vase kept collapsing. It looked more like an ashtray. She thickened the sides, then exclaimed, "Mother! Look what I've made for Father—can you guess what it is?"

"A spittoon," said Freddie, laughing.

"It's a lovely ashtray," Mother said. "Father needs one."

"What do I need?" said a deep voice. Father stood

in the doorway, home early. Katharine thought he was more handsome than any other man in the world.

"An ashtray," said Katharine.

"Er . . . yes . . . I'm sure I do." Father looked embarrassed, and it was only then that Katharine realized he was not alone. Now a woman entered the nursery— a tall woman with gray hair pulled tightly back from a frowning forehead. She was dressed in black; this, and her hooked nose, made Katharine think of a crow. For one second the woman looked with horror at the nursery. Then her face settled into a smile, but one that Katharine instantly did not trust.

Father's eyes shifted around the nursery, too. He pulled at his whiskers. His cheeks were redder than usual, and he was watching the strict-looking lady as if he cared what she thought. He said to Mother, "Diana, here is Miss Pritt. She has arrived a day early."

"Oh, gracious," said Mother. "What a surprise!" She jumped up from the table. A lump of clay fell next to Miss Pritt's black boot. Mother kicked it under the table.

"H-how do you do?" she said. She put out her hand but took it back quickly, shaking her head at her caked fingers. "My goodness. I was planning to tell the children about you tonight."

Miss Pritt said, "I am sorry to have surprised you. I took today's train because recently the trains have been rather unreliable."

Katharine looked with alarm at the stiff black figure.

"We were just making things," said Mother, smiling. Miss Pritt smiled back. Again Katharine saw a frown

7

flicker across her face. She was staring at the slimy gray top of the nursery table and the floor next to Freddie's worktable, which was littered with boards and sawdust.

"Children," said Father. "Come and meet your new nurse." Katharine stomped over to him. "Miss Pritt, this is Katharine."

Miss Pritt's cold, pale eyes rested on her. "I am so happy to meet you, dear child," she said. "We will be great friends." As she smiled, her eyes looked Katharine up and down critically. Katharine noticed that she spoke with an accent.

Father must have read her thoughts, for he said, "Miss Pritt is English. We're very lucky to have her. She has taken care of the children of my friends for many years. Now that their children have grown up, they have suggested that Miss Pritt come to us."

Father motioned to Freddie. "Didn't I tell you to come here?" Freddie looked annoyed to have his work interrupted, but went to Father.

"I'm delighted to have a young man in my care," said Miss Pritt. She gave him a smile that died as she noticed his knickers pockets sagging with nails and a hammer.

"Freddie is making shelves," explained Mother. Freddie still didn't say anything. He was quiet with grown-ups, and kept himself out of trouble that way, while Katharine was often called "headstrong."

"Is your proper name Frederick?" Miss Pritt asked him.

Mother and Father nodded.

"May I call you Frederick?" she asked.

Freddie shrugged.

Miss Pritt turned to Mother and Father. "I'm eager to teach Frederick a little bow—and Katharine a curtsy. Proper manners are very important."

"Excellent," said Father.

Oswald had been hiding behind Mother's skirts.

"Oswald, come forward and greet your nurse," cooed Mother. "Miss Pritt, you'll have the empty room next to Oswald's, on this side of the nursery."

Katharine was aghast. This person was going to live with them! How could Mother and Father have done this without telling her and Freddie?

Oswald waddled over to Miss Pritt with a clay snake in his hand. "Noodle," he said. "Mmmm, noooodle." He opened his mouth.

"Don't you dare," said Miss Pritt in such a firm voice that Oswald stopped, his mouth hanging open. He was accustomed to Mother and Father laughing at whatever he did.

"We don't want Oswald to poison himself," said Miss Pritt, smiling. She began unbuttoning her black gloves. "I say, it's quite clear there's been no nurse here!"

"Er, we're not quite settled," mumbled Father. "We only moved from the country three weeks ago. Now that you're here, Mrs. Outwater will be free to finish decorating the nursery."

"I'll take care of everything, sir," said Miss Pritt. "I'll have the nursery in order in no time. And the children, too."

Katharine was sure of one thing: she didn't want to be put in order—not by a mean nurse.

Father took Mother's arm. "Come with me, Diana. Let's leave Miss Pritt to get acquainted with the children. There's a new shipment of Oriental rugs that just arrived at a Broadway store. Now that Miss Pritt is here, you will be able to see them with me."

"Shouldn't we help Miss Pritt?" asked Mother.

"That's not necessary, madam," said Miss Pritt. "We will manage very well."

"I'll see you later, then," said Mother reluctantly as she was led down the hall by Father. Katharine raced after them.

"What is it, darling?" asked Mother.

Katharine stopped. She felt hurt. She wanted to say, "Don't you want to take care of us anymore?" But instead she whispered, "I don't like her."

"Hush, Katharine. That's not fair," said Mother. "You march right back and get acquainted. Be good. I said I had meant to tell you about Miss Pritt this evening. But it is rude to talk about her behind her back."

Katharine walked slowly back to the nursery and stood beside Freddie and Oswald.

Miss Pritt's smile was gone, and her chest was heaving up and down. "My dear children, I have come to give you a happy and healthy life, teach you how to live according to your social station, and provide you with an education. All this is impossible in such a dirty place!" A look of outrage swept her face. "I am afraid we cannot become better acquainted until we remove all this filth—I will *not* have my nursery in this state."

It's not your nursery, thought Katharine, but she

kept silent. Miss Pritt frightened her. She sneaked Freddie a look of horror. He just winked at her—the same way he had winked when their tutor in the country, Mr. Knapp, became angry at them for not studying. Freddie always managed to get around Mr. Knapp. Now he was telling Katharine they would get around Miss Pritt, too.

"I can't imagine what clay is doing on this table," said Miss Pritt. "Isn't this where we are going to eat?" Miss Pritt took the wastebasket and with one angry motion swept all the clay into it.

"My ashtray," cried Katharine. She knelt by the wastebasket and took it out. The sides were squashed.

"I'm sorry, Katharine. I cannot tolerate this dirt. Please take what you want to your room."

Katharine rescued Mother's vase, which was also crooked now. Hot tears filled her eyes. She hugged the vase and ashtray to her pinafore and went out the nursery's side door into the little hall, then into her room. Freddie's room was next to hers. At the opposite end of the nursery was another little hall and two more bedrooms. One was Oswald's; the other was to belong to Miss Pritt.

Katharine laid the clay down on the night table by her big four-poster bed. The furniture was very dark and heavy for a girl's room. It was Uncle Harry's, and Mother had said she would change it.

Katharine tried to straighten the ashtray and vase through a blur of tears, then dried her eyes on her sleeve. Freddie mustn't see her crying. He had a very low opinion of girls who cried. Besides, she was furious. She hated Miss Pritt. She had never had a nurse and she didn't want one!

There was a banging noise coming from the nursery. Katharine ran to see what it was. Miss Pritt was dragging Freddie's shelves out the door into the hall. The corner had come apart. "Full of germs," she said.

"Miss Pritt, stop!" cried Freddie. He was red in the face, clenching and unclenching his fists.

"I'm sorry, Frederick. We are having a very bad start. But we cannot breathe with sawdust flying in the air. I will not have carpentry in my nursery." Now Miss Pritt was examining the worktable. "That's an old door. Where did you pick it up?"

"I don't remember," said Freddie. "I'm going to speak to my mother about this."

Miss Pritt took his saw between her fingers as if it were a rotten fish and threw it in the hall. Freddie's tools were the only things he had brought from the country. He climbed over the boards in the hall and took the tools to his room.

"I'm telling Mother!" yelled Katharine.

"Your mother is not in charge of this nursery," said Miss Pritt. She smiled at Katharine. "And I'm sure she'll be relieved to hear that there are no germs here."

Just then, the pretty young maid Lottie came in. She flung down a suitcase. "Goodness, why do *I* have to carry this?" she cried. "It's a man's job."

Miss Pritt took the suitcase to her room with only a haughty nod to Lottie.

She needn't unpack, thought Katharine. She's not staying.

When he returned, Freddie was still red in the face. "What's the matter, handsome?" Lottie asked him. She rumpled his hair. "Don't you want to learn some manners from your fancy nurse?"

"No," answered Katharine. Lottie bent over her starched white apron, laughing. She drew two peppermint sticks from her pocket. "Here you are, sweethearts."

Suddenly a tall figure hovered over them. "I'll thank you not to give the children sweets," said Miss Pritt.

"I didn't mean no harm," said Lottie, flushing. She put the peppermint sticks back in her pocket. She seemed to crumple under Miss Pritt's gaze, and left quickly. Katharine thought that was a bad sign.

"Mama!" cried Oswald. There was Mother, in a blue velvet cape, stepping daintily over the lumber. Katharine rushed to her. Oswald flung himself into her arms.

"Mother, look w-what she's done," stammered Freddie. "My tools! My shelves! She says she's getting rid of my worktable."

"That old door is quite filthy, madam. I won't have it in my nursery." Miss Pritt clasped her bony hands. "Poor Frederick is upset. But germs are even more upsetting, aren't they?" She was smiling a sugary smile.

Katharine clung to Mother. Now she was back, everything would be all right. She patted Mother's cloak. When she ran her hand up, it left a dark blue mark. Down, it was smooth and shiny.

"Please, Freddie," said Mother. "Don't look so stricken. Miss Pritt is quite right."

"Oh, Mother," said Freddie. Miss Pritt looked triumphant. "You let me do my carpentry before she came," he said.

"I know, darling." Mother sighed. "That was when we were alone. But I can understand what Miss Pritt means. We'll store your boards and that heavy door in the gardener's shed. When you want to work, you can set the door over two garbage pails in the garden. It will be much better."

"Thank you, madam," said Miss Pritt. "There, Frederick. That will be much better for you."

Mother put Oswald down and took Katharine's arms from her waist. "Father's waiting in the carriage. I must go. Now get acquainted, all of you." Then she was gone.

"Mama!" screamed Oswald. He was only two and he didn't understand. He lay on the floor and sobbed. Miss Pritt stood him on his feet.

"You must know from the beginning—I will not go along with spoiled behavior."

Oswald still sobbed.

Miss Pritt shook him. "No temper tantrums in this nursery," she said.

Katharine gave Freddie another look of horror behind Miss Pritt's back. But when Freddie winked at her this time, he seemed to be blinking back tears. Katharine understood why. Mother had taken sides with this stranger. Mother had betrayed him.

·2·

KATHARINE lay on her bed, kicking at her covers. The curtains were drawn. Miss Pritt was making them have a nap. "I have been a nurse thirty-one years," she said. "I know what's good for you. This is our time for rest and reading, before we go to the park. Let's put our disagreements behind us. Look, I have some books for you. I enjoy very much sharing them with my children." She gave Freddie some thick books to read, and Katharine some fairy tales with beautiful color pictures.

Now that they were in their rooms, Katharine was too angry to look at the book. Naptime—they had given up naps long ago. Wait till she told Mother. She buried her face in her pillow. Mother hadn't listened to Freddie; she had changed. Katharine whispered into her pillow, "Mother doesn't love us anymore. She doesn't want to take care of us. That's why she's gotten a nurse. She doesn't mind if Miss Pritt is mean." Katharine threw her pillow angrily across the room and sat up on the edge of the bed. Mother had always been with them in the country. Katharine had taken it for granted. Unless she was with her own papa, Mother was always ready to play with them.

There had been just Mr. and Mrs. Hodkins in the country. Mr. Hodkins took care of the fields and horses, and Mrs. Hodkins cooked for them. When Mother and Father went to Albany, Mrs. Hodkins stayed in the farmhouse overnight. And of course her twin boys, Clem and Clyde, stayed, too. "Those wild boys," Mrs. Hodkins called them, and sometimes pulled their ears, stretching them way out. The ears stayed red for a long time afterward. But she never scolded Katharine and Freddie.

Mrs. Hodkins had known Katharine since she was born. On the day they left for New York, she had hugged Katharine to her big bosom. "I reckon you could use a batch of my sugar cookies," she said, and thrust a tin into Katharine's hands. "Well, good-bye and God bless you," she said, wiping her tears with the corner of her apron.

Now, instead of Mrs. Hodkins, they had a fat French cook called Eloise who made it clear she didn't want children in her kitchen; and Mr. Sloat and Lottie and many day maids and laundresses; and an old gardener called McSweeney who spat tobacco juice. And a mean nurse.

Katharine flung herself back on her bed. If only they had a puppy, it would make up for moving to the city. Mother had promised. She said, "Then you won't miss the animals in the country so much. As soon as we're settled, we'll get you one." Every day Katharine asked

Mother for the puppy. "Gracious, Katharine, we're not the slightest bit settled yet," Mother always answered.

A puppy would love Katharine. It would cuddle next to her, and she wouldn't feel so alone. She had never had a dog of her own. In the country there had been an old sheepdog that lived in the barn. It loved Mr. Hodkins best because he fed it.

Suddenly Freddie dashed into the room and dived under the bed.

"Freddie! What if Miss Pritt catches you?"

He poked his head out from under the ruffle. "Why, Katharine, you sound afraid of her."

"I'm not," lied Katharine. She felt tears well up in her eyes. "Don't you want Mother to take care of us?"

"Oh, Katharine, you sound like a baby," said Freddie. "I'm too old to 'want Mother,' " he mimicked.

"That's not what I said!" cried Katharine. But it was. She realized she would get no comfort from Freddie.

"I hate Miss Pritt," continued Freddie in a whisper. "I'm going to have my revenge on her—I swear it."

"You sound like King Arthur," said Katharine. Father had been reading them *King Arthur and the Knights of the Round Table*. The knights were always avenging wrongs and defending their ladies' honor. However, Father had stopped in the middle of the story when he became too busy with his business.

There was the sound of footsteps. Freddie ducked under the bed. Katharine lay down and covered her eyes with her arm, pretending to sleep. She peeked out. Her eyes met Miss Pritt's.

"What is your pillow doing on the floor?"

"It fell," said Katharine.

"Across the room? Humph. Pick it up."

Katharine jumped out of bed and picked up the pillow. There was something about Miss Pritt's voice that made her obey.

"Where is Frederick?"

Silence.

Miss Pritt went to the bed and lifted the ruffle. She showed no surprise at seeing Freddie there. She motioned him to crawl out, and led him by the collar back to his room, saying, "I think you had better learn right now to do what I tell you."

Katharine lay still, waiting. She sensed that Miss Pritt was standing in the little hall. She took up her diary and wrote at the bottom of her list:

I hate Miss Pritt.

At last it was time to go to the park. Miss Pritt had Katharine change into a new pink dress, white stockings, a navy jacket, and a most uncomfortable hat with flowers. Freddie had to put on a new suit with a stiff collar and tie and a matching hat, and Oswald wore a sailor suit.

Miss Pritt was prodding Katharine toward the nursery door when Mother suddenly appeared. "Why, how lovely you all look," she said. "Where are you going?"

"To the park in these fancy clothes!" cried Katharine.

Miss Pritt was all smiles. "Her gingham dress was

not presentable," she said. She had called it "disgraceful" to Katharine. "You must excuse us. I believe in lots of fresh air for my children."

"What bad timing," said Mother. "I rushed back from the rug merchant's."

"Mama come," said Oswald. He pulled at her long skirt.

"I must talk to you," begged Katharine.

But Freddie walked right past Mother as if she weren't there. During their nap, Miss Pritt had had his worktable removed.

Miss Pritt said, "We'll see you after supper, madam."

"Oh, I think I'll join you at supper," said Mother. "We'll talk then, Katharine."

Miss Pritt frowned. "I always bring the children down *after* supper, madam."

"Today I'll join you," said Mother. "We must have a little conference together about the children's schedule—"

"Mamaaaa . . ." Oswald clung to Mother's skirts.

Miss Pritt took his hand and Katharine's elbow. Over Oswald's screams she said, "I'm sorry, madam. Surprise visits are *very* disruptive." She pulled Katharine and Oswald into the hall. But Katharine shook off Miss Pritt's cold, bony fingers and ran back to the nursery. Mother was sitting at the nursery table, her chin in her hand. She looked sad.

"Come with us," said Katharine.

Mother just blew her a kiss. "I'll talk to you at supper, I promise," she said. "Go on, now. Be a good girl."

Katharine didn't know how she could survive until supper. It was a long time to wait to ask Mother to send Miss Pritt packing. She followed Miss Pritt down the stairs and out onto the sidewalks of New York. As they passed the stables, Katharine held her nose between her fingers.

"Katharine, that is not ladylike," said Miss Pritt, pushing Oswald's carriage.

Freddie took a lump of sugar from his pocket and fed a truck horse parked on the side of the avenue.

"Frederick!" said Miss Pritt. "You will have that horse's filthy saliva on your hand."

Freddie rinsed his hands in a drinking fountain for horses.

"Do you think that water is clean?" demanded Miss Pritt.

Freddie sighed and wiped his hands on his new trousers.

They turned off Madison on Seventy-first Street, then walked down Fifth Avenue, passing the great stone mansions that faced the park. The mansions belonged to millionaires, and Miss Pritt seemed to know them all.

They walked on and entered Central Park at Sixty-ninth Street. Katharine liked the park—it was almost like the country. It had hills and a meadow with sheep grazing in it, and ponds and a lake, and great rocks as high as hills. At Sixty-fourth Street, the Boys' and Girls' Gate led to the Children's District. They had gone there several times with Mother. It had a sliding rock, worn smooth by so many children sliding down it; and a carousel with wooden horses; and penny goat-cart rides; and toys to be rented from a barnlike building called the Dairy. Below all this was the Menagerie, with a baby hippopotamus and a baby camel and elephants.

Miss Pritt had no intention of going to the Children's District. "It's too long a walk for today. Perhaps we will go another time," she said. On a slope below them was a bench where a stout, white-haired lady dressed in black was sitting. Miss Pritt waved to her.

"Out," said Oswald, who was tied into his carriage.

"Be patient," said Miss Pritt in a cold voice that silenced Oswald. "Now, Katharine and Frederick, listen carefully. My impression is that you have had no discipline in your lives. But now that you are in my charge, I will correct that. You will see how much happier life can be with a little order. So then—here are my rules."

Rules for Central Park? Mother didn't have any.

"I am going to sit over there on the bench," said Miss Pritt. "Do not stray far. I must be able to see you. Do not talk to children you don't know. Remember your social position. You are not to mix with the riffraff that come to this park. Be careful of the bushes, Katharine. They will tear your stockings. Now come along and meet a girl your age and her nurse."

Miss Pritt pushed the carriage down the path and greeted the woman on the bench. "Miss Victory, these are my new charges, Frederick, Katharine, and Oswald Outwater."

Katharine studied the nurse. She looked strict, too.

21

"Katharine. Curtsy if you please," said Miss Pritt. "Frederick, bow like a gentleman." She turned to the nurse. "We apologize for our manners. My children are countrified. You must give them a little time to learn how to greet their elders. Katharine, put one foot behind you and curtsy."

Katharine jerked up and down.

A girl in a yellow dress burst into giggles. Her hair was curled into shiny brown ringlets that shook as she laughed. Katharine felt ashamed. What was wrong?

"This is Amelia Whittaker," said Miss Victory. "I have been her nurse since she was born." She patted the huge yellow bow on top of the girl's head. Amelia was still laughing at Katharine.

Katharine was furious.

"You may play together," said Miss Pritt. "If you follow my rules, another time we will go to the carousel. Run along."

Freddie had brought a stick and small hoop. He practiced catching the hoop with the stick while Katharine and Amelia watched. Katharine felt suddenly shy. Amelia was the first city girl she had met. She felt Amelia staring at her, and pushed her flowery hat back.

"Did you use curlpapers?" asked Amelia. "I've never seen such curly hair."

"No," said Katharine, surprised by the question. Now she knew how Amelia had gotten those tight ringlets.

Freddie came up to them. "Let's play tag," he said. "I'll be it. Go on." After counting to ten, he chased Amelia. She was easy to catch. Of course, thought

Katharine. Who could run in all those frills and petticoats?

Amelia was it for a long time. To escape her, Katharine just had to run into the bushes.

"That's not fair," called Amelia. "I don't want to spoil my dress in there." Finally Freddie slowed down and let Amelia tag him.

"You can't catch me!" yelled Katharine. But suddenly Miss Pritt's black form interfered with her escape.

"Katharine, young ladies do not shout. You sound like a peddler in the street. The park is for the enjoyment of nature."

Then Freddie tagged Katharine. "That's not fair," she said in as quiet a voice as she could manage, and was off. She gave Amelia only a halfhearted chase, but Amelia said she wasn't playing.

After a while Freddie quit the game and walked toward some giant rocks that rose in the distance. Katharine looked to see if Miss Pritt had noticed. She had been joined by other nurses and was busy talking while Oswald waddled nearby. Several baby carriages were parked next to them.

Katharine headed for the rocks. One side was sheer cliff. She and Freddie had started rock climbing since coming to New York. Freddie was dreaming of conquering the Himalayas one day. So was Katharine, although she wasn't sure girls got to climb the Himalayas.

Amelia caught up with her. "Where are you going?" she asked.

"I'm going to climb those rocks."

"You'll rip your stockings."

"I don't care," said Katharine.

"Your hat's crooked," said Amelia.

Katharine threw the hat on the grass. She started up the steep rock after Freddie, squeezing her high-buttoned shoes and her fingers into cracks and tiny ledges. She would show that stuck-up Amelia how a country girl could climb. At last she lifted one knee over the top. What was Freddie staring at? She stood up, proud that she had made it, and turned around.

Below was Miss Pritt, looking small from their height, waving her arms like a crow. "Come down this instant! Ladies do not climb rocks. Frederick, you will ruin your new suit."

Amelia walked over to Miss Pritt and handed her Katharine's hat. She pointed up and said, "Look. She's ripped her stocking."

Katharine looked down and saw a large hole in her stocking at her knee. That girl cared too much about clothes. Katharine was sure she could never be friends with her.

Freddie said, "Miss Pritt doesn't let us do anything!" But suddenly his eyes twinkled. "Let's really upset her. We'll pretend we're stuck."

They started down the sheer face of the cliff, stopping on a narrow ledge halfway down.

"Miss Pritt, we can't get down. Help," Freddie called.

"Help!" cried Katharine.

Miss Pritt was beside herself. A small crowd gathered. Some elegant ladies with lacy parasols and men in bowler hats stopped their walk to watch. Miss Pritt said, "This is my first day with these children. I had no idea they were so wild."

Katharine was thrilled with the embarrassment they had caused Miss Pritt. While they made their way down the cliff, she whispered, "We'll tell Mother everything at supper, and she'll send Miss Pritt away."

"She won't listen," said Freddie, shaking his head. "Father won't, either. Because they want you to be a lady, and me a gentleman. They've changed, Katharine. They expect us to change, too."

·3·

MOTHER didn't come to the nursery for supper. Katharine kept her eyes on the door as she sat at the table, a plate of chicken and string beans in front of her. She was so disappointed, she could hardly eat.

It was a quiet supper, except for Miss Pritt. "Oswald, keep your mouth shut. We do not wish to have a view of everything you are eating. Frederick, take your elbows *off* the table. Katharine, I see why you are skin and bones. You must not be such a fussy eater."

What a lot of rules! Katharine had so much to tell Mother. After their cliff-hanging escapade in Central Park, Katharine had heard Miss Pritt complain to Miss Victory, "These children are so ill-bred. I don't know where to begin. I will have to make a lot of changes until things are done *my* way."

Katharine sighed and pushed some chicken skin to the side of her plate. Miss Pritt was not going to excuse her until it was all eaten. Finally she swallowed the last piece and felt it settle, like a lump, in her stomach.

Miss Pritt took out her watch. It was six o'clock. According to her schedule, it was time for Katharine and Freddie to visit Mother and Father in the drawing room. Miss Pritt had them wash up as if they were going to see visitors. Freddie ran ahead.

"Katharine, change your stockings," said Miss Pritt.

But Katharine was already down the stairs. She burst through the paneled doors of the drawing room. "Mother! Father!"

"Here we are, Katharine," said Father, smiling. "No need to look so alarmed. We didn't run away." He and Mother were seated on a velvet sofa in the middle of the large room. It looked rich even to Katharine, who didn't care about such things. Its chandelier sent glittering specks of light over the satin and silk sofas and chairs; heavy brocade curtains hung on either side of the tall windows. Every table was covered with lace or embroidered cloth and was crowded with figurines, boxes with inlaid jewels, vases, and lamps with beaded shades. There was a marble fireplace at one end of the room, and many Oriental rugs overlapped one another on the floor.

A silver tea set was on the low table in front of her parents. "Mother, you didn't come for supper," said Katharine.

"Mother had to call on some friends with me," said Father. "And Miss Pritt needs time alone to get settled with you. Never mind. Look at you—what a little lady Miss Pritt has made of you already!"

Oswald waddled in and climbed onto Mother's lap. Freddie stood apart, scowling.

"And you boys look like perfect little gentlemen," exclaimed Father.

Miss Pritt smiled as she stood by the paneled doors.

"Miss Pritt didn't let me climb rocks or trees—" started Katharine.

"Don't point, Katharine," said Mother.

"I see you still managed to do some damage to your stockings," said Father, laughing. "Come and sit next to me, Katharine. It's good to see you dressed up for a change." Katharine sat down, and Father put his arm around her.

"Miss Pritt, why don't you relax a little?" said Mother. "Have a nice cup of tea in the pantry."

"Very well, madam." Miss Pritt withdrew, closing the paneled doors.

"She made us take a nap," cried Katharine. "And I had to eat everything on my plate when I wasn't even hungry and—"

"I don't see any harm in that," said Father. "You look too thin."

"And we're always having to wash up," added Katharine. This made Father chuckle.

"I hate her!" said Katharine, furious that Father was laughing and Mother was so quiet. *"And I hate Uncle Harry most of all!"*

"Really, Katharine." Father took his arm from around her and gave her an exasperated look. "Kindly leave Uncle Harry out of this." He sighed, as if he had been over all this before. "We stayed too long in the country, I can see that. You are country bumpkins."

He stood up and smiled down at Katharine. "Miss Pritt is going to teach you to be a lady."

"She's awful and I don't want to be a lady!" shouted Katharine. She wished Freddie would speak up. "Freddie thinks she's really mean."

Freddie said, "Oswald's been crying a lot."

Mother sighed and hugged Oswald. She only cares about her baby, Katharine thought. She doesn't care about me anymore.

Father looked tired. "We need your help, children," he said. "I've worked hard to build my reputation as a lawyer in Albany. Now I want to make my mark in New York. I'm working in my own office, trying to find new clients. Meanwhile, I've got my eye on the oldest and best firm in New York. But I won't just get invited to join. Mother and I must see many people, and so must you. I need your best manners. That's why Miss Pritt is here."

Father walked over to Freddie. "Let's hear from you. I doubt a big man like you is going to be bothered by Miss Pritt. She is going to help you with your studies so that you can enter the New York Boys' Academy next autumn."

Freddie shifted from foot to foot. Katharine knew he was looking forward to playing baseball at the academy, and he couldn't resist being called a "big man." He shrugged. "I don't care," he said, "as long as she lets me do my carpentry."

"She will," said Mother.

Father returned to the sofa and looked down at Katharine. "Miss Pritt is going to give you lessons, too," he said. "Your mother has heard of an excellent new school for girls, but you've hardly been prepared for it. I'm afraid Mr. Knapp had no control over you."

"Miss Pritt comes very highly recommended to us," said Mother. "You must give her a chance. Katharine, you've gotten off on the wrong foot with her. We are told she is the *best* nurse in New York City. At least we know you are in safe hands with her when we go out. Remember when you and Freddie got lost in Central Park? What a fright I had until the nice police officer brought you home. This is not the country. We do not know everybody, but I won't worry if Miss Pritt is with you. I can go out with peace of mind."

That was all Katharine heard of all the speeches. Mother and Father were going to leave them more often than ever. Father got up as if he considered the matter closed. Katharine was very disappointed, especially after all her plans to have Miss Pritt sent packing.

"Then get us a puppy, please," she said.

"What?" asked Father.

"Oh, Katharine, you know we're not settled yet," replied Mother. "Think what a puppy would do to our new rugs."

"You will love New York just as we do," said Father, smiling broadly at Katharine and Freddie. He left the drawing room.

Mother reached under the fringe of the sofa and brought out a box of chocolate bonbons. Katharine was almost too upset to take one, but she and Freddie loved sweets, and they ended up eating several of the soft, delicious chocolates.

"Now, Katharine, you mustn't be stubborn," said Mother. "Freddie, please don't be angry. I have a wonderful idea. Let's play hide-and-seek. Uncle Harry's house is perfect for it. Freddie, you and Katharine go hide. Oswald and I will find you."

Katharine and Freddie played reluctantly at first, but soon started to enjoy the game. Uncle Harry's house had so many hiding places—in massive cabinets, behind fringed curtains and marble statues. Mother had to give up several times. When she and Oswald hid, he usually called out, "Fweddie! Katwin!" which made them all laugh. After a while Freddie took Katharine up to the servants' quarters on the fourth floor, then up the narrow stairs to the attic, lit dimly by a small window that let in the evening light.

Freddie dived behind a trunk. Katharine tripped on a suitcase and flew over it, banging herself hard against the lower wall. Her shoulder and elbow ached, but she paid no attention because *the wall was moving*. Part of the wall swung open a few inches and began to close. She put her hand in to stop it. It was a door about three feet high, attached at the corner of the attic by a hidden hinge. Its other side, which she was holding, was cut unevenly, according to where the boards ended, so that it looked ragged. Katharine realized immediately that if the door was closed, there would be no sign of it in the wall—no doorknob, no hinge.

She pulled the door wide; in the gloomy attic light

she saw a little room behind the opening. "Freddie," she gasped. "I've found a secret room."

Freddie crawled over. "What secret—" He stopped. "A secret room!"

The next moment they had crawled in. The room was about eight feet square, with a slanted ceiling. Opposite the door they would not be able to stand.

"No one's been here in ages," said Freddie. "Look at these cobwebs."

Suddenly the door shut and they were in total darkness.

"Freddie, help!"

"Why did you let go of the door?"

"You did! How are we going to get out?"

"Calm down, Katharine. Feel for a knob. . . . There must be one."

Katharine ran her hands over the walls, no longer sure which one had opened to let them in. She banged the lower boards, hoping they would move. Stringy cobwebs stuck to her fingers. She imagined herself locked away for days.

Then she noticed a bare sliver of light. She lunged for it and banged her head painfully on the ceiling. But her hand felt a little square of wood. She pulled. It moved, and with it part of the wall. She had opened a window, or rather an opening in the wall, without glass. The pale evening light filled the room.

"Oh, thank goodness," she cried. Freddie knelt beside her. They looked out at the garden and the neighbors' gardens below. The window was partly covered by vines that grew over that part of the house.

"I think someone planted those vines on purpose," said Freddie. "Just to hide this window. I wonder who built this room."

"Do you think it was Uncle Harry?"

"Maybe he has hidden treasure under a board."

"Or a skeleton," suggested Katharine, who had the lowest opinion of Uncle Harry.

"We'll come back," said Freddie. "But let's get out of here now before someone discovers us." He crawled to the wall opposite the window and examined the lower boards in the fading light. "Look, here's the door. Oh, it's so clever. The hinges are in the corner, and here's the knob." He pushed a little square of wood on the lowest board. *Click.* The door opened.

"Oh, Katharine, what a splendid discovery!" he exclaimed. "It's just what we need. Quick, close the window and come out. We don't want anyone else to know about this."

They crawled out and admired how the door fit back into the wall. Freddie tapped the lowest board, but the door didn't reopen. "It has to be hit hard, and no one's going to do that," he said. "No one's going to discover this. It's just luck that you did, Katharine."

"I know," said Katharine, rubbing her sore elbow where a bump had formed.

"It's ours," whispered Freddie, and he hugged Katharine—something he had not done in years. They pushed a trunk in front of the secret door and ran down the stairs.

"Don't tell *anyone,*" said Freddie.

"Not even Mother?"

Freddie stopped short, so that Katharine bumped into him. "Of course not."

They came upon Mother and Miss Pritt in the third-floor hallway.

"We've been looking all over for you," said Mother. "You hid too well. Miss Pritt came for you, and I had to tell her there were two missing children. Where were you?"

"In a closet," said Freddie.

"Goodness, it must have been a very dirty closet. Your hands are black."

"That's what comes of playing games all over the house," said Miss Pritt.

Freddie moved closer to Mother. He had suddenly forgiven her.

Miss Pritt drew out her watch, which was attached to a chain in her pocket. "Madam, it's time for the children to get ready for bed. Permit me to get them washed."

"Oh?" Mother looked confused. "I usually put the children to bed."

"Ah, you needn't bother, madam. You will be able to dress for your dinner engagement."

When they were in their nightclothes, Miss Pritt brought a table from her room and a wooden box. "And now, children, we have time for something special. It sharpens your eyes and helps you concentrate, too."

She put chairs next to the table and had Katharine and Freddie sit before she opened the box. Inside were hundreds of tiny wooden pieces of a puzzle, mostly green and light blue. "It's a scene from the English countryside. Let's see how you do. My other children did a puzzle very much like this when they were younger than you—it took them half a year."

"It won't take me that long," said Freddie, who liked puzzles, "but I've never seen so many pieces." He and Katharine separated the tiny blue pieces from the green ones as Miss Pritt watched. Katharine let her thoughts wander to the mysterious room she had discovered.

Freddie had managed only to fit a few corner pieces together before Miss Pritt sent them to bed. A little while later Mother breezed into Katharine's darkened room. She wore a satin gown and had gardenias pinned to her hair. Father was behind her in white tie and formal tailcoat.

"*Now* where are you going?" demanded Katharine.

"To a dinner party of some very dull people," said Mother. "I wish I were staying with you."

"Don't go, then!" said Katharine, sitting up. She handed Father *King Arthur* from her night table. "Read to us, Father."

"I'm afraid I spent too long tonight on a confounded law case," he said. "*King Arthur* will have to wait."

Mother and Father kissed Katharine, and then they were gone. For a long time afterward the sweet smell of gardenias lingered in the room. Katharine couldn't understand why her parents would leave her for a party with people they didn't even like.

"Pssst." Freddie was standing in her doorway. "I'm making plans. We're going to fix up"—he broke off to check for Miss Pritt—"the secret room. We're going to build furniture together. If we find treasure under a board, it's ours—oh!" Miss Pritt loomed behind him.

"Well, just as I expected. You are not getting enough sleep. That is why you look sickly, Katharine. You need a proper schedule. Order in one's life makes for order in one's mind. Come along, Frederick. Goodnight." Miss Pritt grasped the collar of Freddie's nightshirt and marched him to his room.

Katharine lay down again, excited. She and Freddie had a secret room. She was very pleased with herself for having discovered it. Freddie was making plans, and she was in them! They might even find treasure. Then, if things got too terrible, they could run away. Mother and Father would probably be at a dinner party and wouldn't even know their children were missing.

·4·

THE NEXT MORNING Freddie pulled Katharine into his room. "I've thought of the perfect way to distract Miss Pritt," he said.

"What do you mean by 'distract'?" asked Katharine.

"Get her attention off us. In this case, off *me*. You'll do it. Now listen—I'll tie a few knots in your hair, and you ask Miss Pritt to comb it for you. That should keep her busy. Meanwhile, I'll go look for treasure." He handed Katharine his comb.

"But I want to go, too," she said, "and I never comb my hair. It's too tangled."

"That's the whole point," said Freddie. "Please, Katharine. You'll go up next time. Please."

Katharine wasn't used to Freddie begging. "Oh, all right," she said, and let him tie knots in her hair. It felt good; she liked having her hair played with. Then Freddie left, carrying a white towel with an embroidered "O" for "Outwater" to use for a little cleaning.

Katharine walked into the nursery. "Oh, Miss Pritt, my hair is all tangled," she blurted out. "Will you please help me comb it?" She handed Miss Pritt the comb.

"I've been wanting to get a comb through that frizz," said Miss Pritt. She sat Katharine down at the window seat and began to yank at a tangled clump of hair.

"Owwwww," groaned Katharine. And soon she said, "Let's not bother. Mother always brushes my hair. Stop it!"

"Sit still. Your mother let your hair go frizzy by not combing it."

Katharine's eyes were swimming with tears. Freddie's comb lost several teeth in its struggle through her curls. How many knots had Freddie tied, anyway? It was ages before Miss Pritt threw away the broken comb and went to Oswald's room. Katharine tiptoed to the little hall and peeked in.

"Get dressed," Miss Pritt was saying.

"Pooh," answered Oswald, and put his pants on his head. Mother always laughed at this.

"You are no longer a baby, so do not act like one."

Oswald lay down and started bawling. Katharine ran down the hall. She was sorry for Oswald, but she could tell he was going to distract Miss Pritt for some time. She took the attic stairs two at a time and banged her way into the secret room.

"Katharine!" exclaimed Freddie. "Warn me before you come bursting in like that." The window was open. He was on his knees, dusting the walls with the towel. "What are you doing here? Where's Miss Pritt?"

"She's with Oswald. He's having a tantrum. And I

should be, too. You put me through a dreadful torture!"

"I'm sorry," said Freddie. "Your hair does look pretty."

"That's not funny." Katharine looked around. The secret room seemed very pleasant in the daylight. Bright patches of sunlight came through the vine-covered window and onto the floor. "There's no treasure?" she asked.

"No. I looked for loose boards; I banged everywhere . . . poked in every knot." Freddie didn't sound very disappointed. "Doesn't the room look bigger in the daylight? There's lots of space for furniture. We'll build a table first. This will be our hideaway from everyone downstairs."

"From the mean old witch," said Katharine, jumping up and bumping her head on the ceiling.

"Shhhhh!"

They took turns wiping the cobwebs off the walls. Although they would never have dusted their rooms downstairs, here they fought over the towel. They left it, as black as it had once been white, in an old valise in the attic, and returned to the nursery.

They were just in time. Miss Pritt entered with Oswald, who was finally dressed.

"Look at you," she said. "Standing there gaping with nothing to do. I must speak to your mother. You should be studying—this is our time for lessons. But there isn't even a piece of lined paper in the nursery."

They hadn't been missed! Katharine picked up Oswald and hugged him. He had red blotches around his eyes from crying.

"Miss Pritt, then can we please go down to the garden?" asked Freddie.

"Not 'can'—'*may*' we go. And yes, I suppose you may as well."

They raced down to the garden. It had a patch of grass in the center, with flower beds around it and high walls. A stone pool was in one corner. Uncle Harry must have had fish in it, but now it held only dirty water.

Katharine and Freddie dragged two garbage pails onto the grass from the alley between their house and the next, and placed the old door over them. Freddie's vise was still in place. They brought the boards from behind the toolshed, and Freddie measured them and marked them with a pencil. He was very nice to Katharine, who wasn't used to him insisting that she use the saw first, or to him asking her advice.

"How high should the table be?" he asked.

"Hmmmm. . . . It should be low."

"Yes, exactly. We'll sit on the floor. The ceiling's not high enough for chairs," said Freddie.

They looked up at Uncle Harry's house, trying to find the outline of the window of the secret room. Under the slanting roof, the top of the building was wood and covered with vines. There was no sign of the window.

Katharine and Freddie smiled happily at each other. They were so absorbed in their work they didn't see two figures approaching.

"Madam, what will the neighbors think?" Miss Pritt's voice made Katharine jump. Mother was with her, dressed to go out, in a short jacket and a hat with a tall feather. "It looks disgraceful—garbage pails in the garden."

"Mother, you said we could work here," cried Freddie. "We're making a bedside table."

"We don't even know the neighbors," shouted Katharine.

"Katharine, if you're not quiet, I expect all the neighbors will know us," said Mother. She looked at Miss Pritt. "The boy is a builder," she said. "He was always making something in the country. I'm delighted they have found something to do. Besides, they'll get plenty of fresh air. I know you are very much in favor of that."

Mother started to walk away with Miss Pritt. "We've left Oswald with Lottie so that Miss Pritt and I can have a little conference," she told Katharine and Freddie.

"To plan every minute of our lives," whispered Katharine.

"Good-bye, darlings," called Mother. "I'm going to buy you readers and spellers and arithmetic books and your very own notebooks."

Katharine didn't want her very own notebook. She dreaded lessons with Miss Pritt. She held on to the boards and Freddie hammered. But it wasn't long before they were interrupted again.

McSweeney, the old gardener, stood over them in his dirty overalls and floppy hat, and breathed down on them with his tobacco breath. "What's them trash cans doin' in my garden?" he demanded.

"We have my parents' permission," said Freddie, without looking up. He hammered furiously, and Katharine kept her thumbs as out of his way as possible.

"I won't have it," said McSweeney. "Them trash cans is killing my grass."

Freddie hammered more furiously. Katharine removed not only her thumbs but all her fingers.

McSweeney spat on his grass. Katharine tried to ignore him. She remembered that Mother didn't like him much; Mother said he had come with the house and acted as if the garden belonged to him. At last he moved away to weed his beds of roses.

"We can't even make a table without everyone trying to stop us," said Freddie. "But we'll do it. We'll use every free moment we get."

There were not many of those. In the next two days Miss Pritt established the routine that was to make them so happy and healthy. "You are crying out for order," she said. The schedule was lessons in the morning (but thank goodness the books had not yet arrived); lunch; nap and reading time; a walk to the park and play there; supper; a visit to Mother and Father in the drawing room; and, at bedtime, work on the puzzle. There was also washing up—morning, noon, and night.

Somehow Katharine and Freddie found time to work on the table in between all of these activities. It took two days to cut the wood and hammer it together, and to reinforce the legs with extra wood so the table wouldn't wobble. They wanted the table to be perfect.

On the third day Mother had only to start a whispered conference with Miss Pritt for Katharine and Freddie to dash down to the garden and start sanding the table smooth. Too soon, however, Mother and Miss Pritt came down to tell them to put everything away. "We are taking you shopping for a proper wardrobe," said Mother.

Katharine was beginning to tire of the word "proper."

They went by horse cab to the fashionable shops and huge emporiums between Ninth and Twenty-third streets on Broadway. Mother told them this was the famous Ladies' Mile. First they went to a tailor for Freddie, then a dressmaker for Katharine. The dressmaker also made baby clothes for Oswald. Their last stop was Mother's milliner, to choose some hats for Katharine. In the window were hats on high sticks.

"I'll wait outside," said Freddie, who was in a horrid mood. He hated to shop.

"You choose them for me," said Katharine, but Mother took her arm and led her inside. Miss Pritt followed with Oswald. They were greeted by a short man whose stiff, waxed mustache stood straight out from his cheeks. He bowed low to Mother.

"Mrs. Outwater, what an honor."

"I've brought my daughter to you," Mother answered. "She is in great need of some proper hats."

The man bowed to Katharine and looked her up and down. "Very charming, but madam, does she look more like Mr. Outwater?" he asked.

Mother hugged Katharine. "No, no, when I was young, I looked just like her." She must have noted Katharine's look of disbelief, because she said to her, "It's a pity I have no photographs of myself very young."

Then Katharine was surrounded by shop girls in white shirtwaists. Hats were put on her—straw boaters and hats with wide brims and ribbons and flowers. Mother consulted Miss Pritt often.

"Katharine, which ones do you like?" Mother asked.

Katharine whispered in her ear, "I hate them all."

"All right, dear," said Mother, blushing, and keeping a frozen smile on her lips.

At last the ordeal was over. They decided to take a streetcar uptown because Oswald wanted to. Mother gave Freddie and Katharine a nickel each to pay the conductor, and the streetcar started its fast pace uptown. Katharine stood in the middle aisle with Freddie, hanging on to a strap she could barely reach, although there were many empty seats. Mother sat with Oswald in her lap. Miss Pritt sat very stiffly on the opposite side of the aisle.

Katharine bent over to Mother. "If you weren't here, she wouldn't let me stand and hold the strap. She doesn't let me do anything—"

"Katharine," said Mother, squeezing her arm firmly. "What if she hears you? That is plain rude. You must try to get on with her. I will not listen to any more complaints, and that is final."

Mother doesn't love me anymore, thought Katharine. She didn't enjoy the rest of the ride.

Mother left them to do more errands, and Miss Pritt took over. It was only later in the day, after they had been to the park, that Katharine and Freddie could finish sanding their table.

The next day they spread Father's newspapers on the grass, then painted the table white with paint from McSweeney's toolshed. By bedtime the paint was dry, and the table was finished. It had taken four days to make.

"It's splendid!" they both said. But they had no idea how they were going to get it up to the secret room. They carried it to Freddie's room because they had told everyone they were making him a bedside table. It looked short and silly next to his high bed.

Before going to the opera, Father and Mother came in with Miss Pritt to see the table.

"Why, it's nice," said Mother weakly.

"We'll have to cut the legs off your bed to fit the table," said Father, teasing. "Next time, think things through more carefully." He ruffled Freddie's hair.

Freddie took the criticism but became red in the face. "We're going to make bookshelves next," he said.

"That is all very well," said Father, "but it's time for you children to concentrate on your studies."

Freddie was playing with Father's top hat, first collapsing it and then making it spring open. Father asked for it back and put it on his head. "It's safer here," he said, and laughed. "Now I have time for a page or two of *King Arthur*."

They sat on Freddie's bed and Father read to them. Katharine didn't always understand the story, but she loved Father's deep, steady voice and she loved to cuddle close to him. He didn't read with his usual force, perhaps because Miss Pritt was standing stiffly at the end of the bed, frowning at her watch.

Three pages were over very quickly. Mother and Father rushed out, leaving King Arthur in the midst of another joust, and Miss Pritt to put them to bed.

Katharine lay in bed, feeling sad. Then she started worrying about the table they had worked so hard to make. Miss Pritt might have it thrown away. The clay vase and ashtray had disappeared, and Katharine was certain Miss Pritt had removed them.

Suddenly Freddie was in her room. "They won't make fun of our table after tonight," he whispered.

"Why?"

"Because we're going to take it up in the middle of the night."

"What?"

"Good-night," he said loudly. Miss Pritt had appeared behind him.

After that, Katharine stared up at the ceiling, too excited to sleep. She didn't dare call out to Freddie, certain that Miss Pritt was hovering by their doors. When would she go to her own room?

Katharine waited impatiently for the middle of the night.

"Katharine, wake up." Freddie was tapping her shoulder.

Katharine sat bolt upright. "What time is it?" she asked, rubbing her eyes.

"Two o'clock. I heard the chimes. Mother and Father came back some time ago. I've got an old kerosene lamp of Uncle Harry's and matches. The table's in the hall. Come on!"

They each took an end of the table, tiptoed down the hall, then stopped. They hurried back to listen by Miss Pritt's door. They heard the faint sound of regular breathing. Katharine's heart was pounding.

Then they carried the table down the long, dark hall to the stairs to the fourth floor. Freddie had the unlit lamp in one hand and one end of the table in his other. Katharine followed with the table gripped tightly in both hands. A small hall lamp glowed at the other end of the hall by Father's and Mother's rooms. Huge, moving shadows spread up the walls like monsters. At first they frightened Katharine; then she realized they were Freddie's and her own. The house was full of creaking noises she never heard during the day. She looked over her shoulder every few steps, half expecting Miss Pritt to pounce.

The table was a heavy load to carry up the stairs. One corner hit the wall, and they stopped, gasping. But the noise did not seem to have wakened anybody.

They stopped on the fourth floor. One of the servants was snoring loudly. Katharine whispered, "Maybe we shouldn't go up."

"Are you going to be a coward?"

"No."

They felt their way up the steep, dusky attic stairs, which squeaked terribly. At the top they found themselves in complete darkness.

"Put the table down, gently," said Freddie. He struck a match. The light cast deep shadows on his face. Katharine pushed the trunk away from the secret door and gave the lower boards as soft a bang as possible. It sounded like a gun going off. The door opened.

"Wait!" Freddie blew out the match, which had burned down to his fingers. He lit another. They crawled in, and Freddie lit the kerosene lamp. It bathed every corner of the room in a yellow-orange light. Freddie moved it by the window but did not let it touch the wall. "We have to be very careful not to start a fire," he said.

"It's so wonderful to be back in our cozy room!" exclaimed Katharine.

They had to open the door again to bring in the table. It barely fit through the door and scraped noisily as they pulled it in. They placed it against the wall under the window and sat facing each other on either side of it, their legs underneath.

"It's perfect," said Freddie.

After they had admired it, Katharine said, "I'm going to make curtains for the window. Pretty, frilly ones out of that new petticoat with all the scratchy lace layers they bought for me!"

"That's a good idea," said Freddie. He opened the window an inch so that the fresh night air came in.

"Oh, Freddie, your nightshirt's getting dirty," said Katharine. "Miss Pritt's going to wonder where we've been. We really must clean up here."

"I'll go and get a pail of water and some rags," said Freddie.

"Now?"

"It's the best time in the world. It's the only time we have that is not scheduled by Miss Pritt."

He opened the door and was gone. Katharine sat listening to strange noises in the walls. She opened the window wide until she realized that someone in a nearby building might see the secret window.

Freddie was quickly back with a mop, a pail of water, and rags. "Everyone's snoring away," he said. "It sounds like a beehive."

They scrubbed the walls and were thrilled to discover yellow-brown wood under the grime. Katharine mopped the floor. Soon the water, the rags, and their nightclothes were black.

"I'll slip our nightgowns to a laundress tomorrow," said Katharine.

"I think we should make shelves next," said Freddie. "We need them. We're going to store things here—games and food. We'll leave this lamp."

"What if it's missed?"

"It doesn't matter," said Freddie, grinning. "No one will ever find it. Let's go."

He carefully blew out the lamp. They crawled through the secret door and made sure it was closed tightly. Then they stumbled down the attic stairs with the pail and mop and rags. On the fourth floor Katharine whispered, "I've got this feeling that Miss Pritt is in the hall downstairs, waiting to attack us."

"Don't be silly," said Freddie. But he left the cleaning things in the middle of the fourth-floor hall instead of putting them away. And they raced down the stairs, hardly worrying about the noise, and dived into their beds. Katharine lay panting, her heart thumping in her ears.

Silence.

She jumped out of bed, and before changing into a new nightdress, she tiptoed into Freddie's room. "We made it!" she whispered. "This is fun!"

And Freddie answered, "It's the most fun we've had in ages."

·5·

IN THE MORNING Katharine sat at the nursery table, facing a very soft-boiled egg and Miss Pritt. Miss Pritt's bony hands were folded. Katharine knew she was willing to sit as long as it would take for the egg to be eaten.

Katharine put some yellow slime on her fork. Whitish uncooked egg hung down. She put it in her mouth.

"Who dumped my mop and pail outside my room?" demanded Lottie, storming into the room.

Katharine choked.

"They're filthy," cried Lottie. "Whoever took 'em could at least clean 'em and put 'em away!"

"I'll thank you not to speak to me in that tone of voice," said Miss Pritt while she slapped Katharine's back to stop her fit of coughing. She waved Lottie away. Then she filled a spoon with egg and pressed it into Katharine's mouth.

Katharine gagged. The last spoonful Katharine fed herself.

"Very good," said Miss Pritt. "That egg will

51

strengthen you. Stay right where you are. We're going to start your lessons." Miss Pritt left the breakfast things on a tray outside for Lottie to pick up, and went to get Freddie from his room. "I see you've gotten rid of your bedside table," she said.

"Yes, we threw it out this morning," said Freddie. "It *was* too low. We're going to make bookshelves instead."

"Humph! I expect your mother will buy you *proper* furniture."

Miss Pritt opened two notebooks. Into these she had Katharine and Freddie copy the sentence "Wisdom is more precious than rubies."

"A noble thought for beginning our studies," said Miss Pritt.

They dipped their pens in the ink. Katharine had hardly started writing when Miss Pritt said, "What wild letters—going in every direction. And you haven't even dotted all your *i*'s, not that I'm surprised. It's the writing of an undisciplined child."

Freddie fared better. He had tiny writing, so his sloppiness didn't show up. Mr. Knapp hadn't bothered much with penmanship.

Miss Pritt gave Katharine a thick reader. Katharine read it out loud for Miss Pritt in her slow fashion until Miss Pritt cried, "Enough!" as if she couldn't bear to hear Katharine stumble on another word. "This is only the Third Reader," she said. "You will be entering the fourth class. You are way behind city children. Do you realize it?"

In the middle of Freddie's reading Miss Pritt exclaimed, "Poor pronunciation, Frederick. You just said 'dis*up*pear' for 'dis*ap*pear.' You should read with expression—raise your voice for some parts, lower it for others." She shook her head. "When you read out loud at school, they will laugh you off the platform."

They both gaped at her.

"Have you had your multiplication tables, Katharine?" Miss Pritt asked next.

"What?"

"Frederick, what is twelve times eleven? Quick!"

"One hundred eleven," said Freddie.

"Humph. You are wrong, Frederick. You both should know your multiplication tables like that." She snapped her fingers under their noses. "Frederick, you need to learn fractions. Katharine, you must work hard or you will be the dunce of that newfangled school your mother wants you to attend. I understand Amelia Whittaker is being sent there next fall, too. As if young ladies needed to go to school. Humph!"

During the next three hours, Miss Pritt developed the lowest opinion of Mr. Knapp. Still, she ended the lesson with a smile. "Fortunately I can help you. We are going to work *very* hard." She seemed eager to help them.

They were excused to go down to the garden to start their shelves. They had done more work in one day with Miss Pritt than in a month with Mr. Knapp.

"Are we really so far behind?" Katharine asked Freddie as they started sawing his remaining lumber.

"I don't know," said Freddie. Katharine thought he looked worried.

"I hope Miss Pritt doesn't tell Father," said Katharine.

But she did. Father was away for a couple of days on a business trip. But the evening he returned, Miss Pritt brought Katharine's and Freddie's notebooks down to the drawing room. She placed them in front of Mother and Father.

"I'm sorry to report that the children's education up to now has been a disaster," she said. She didn't sound sorry at all. "I will do everything I can, I assure you. I've brought you some of my lesson plans."

"Thank you for your efforts," said Father to Miss Pritt. "We are very grateful."

"Sir, I have given Frederick stories by Dickens and Sir Walter Scott to read in his free time, instead of those cheap dime novels in his room. It is important to read only good books that give a true picture of men and women."

"Excellent," said Father. "I liked Dickens as a boy."

Katharine nudged Freddie in the ribs. She knew how he loved his adventure books. She guessed some of them would be given a safe home up in the secret room.

When Miss Pritt had gone, Father shook his head. "It's just as I suspected," he said. "You two wound Mr. Knapp around your little fingers and accomplished nothing. Now you are ill-prepared for the challenge of New York." His face brightened. "At least we have Miss Pritt."

"We hate her lessons!" said Katharine. "It's drill,

drill, drill, and writing noble thoughts a hundred times."

Father chuckled. "I didn't like my studies either, when I was young."

Mother passed around little seedcakes. "Let's have a treat. Katharine and Freddie, I've been watching you the last two days, busy as beavers in the garden. What are you making now? I couldn't quite tell from the window."

"We were making bookshelves, but"—Freddie shrugged—"they didn't work out at all."

"That's a pity," said Mother.

"They fell apart," said Katharine. She looked Mother straight in the eye, too, just as Freddie had. She had never lied to Mother before. The truth was, the bookshelves were made and painted white, and looked beautiful. They were hidden behind the toolshed, waiting to be taken up to the secret room.

"Katharine, you have changed," said Mother. "You seem very busy and content. Isn't that so, Father? We've been sitting here for some time, and Katharine hasn't complained about New York or Miss Pritt—except for her *lessons,* and that's only natural. I do believe she is getting used to life here."

"I *am not!*" cried Katharine. "You just want to think everything is all right, but it isn't." She was hurt that Mother had seen her and Freddie in the garden and hadn't bothered to join them.

"Mama. Papa. Find!" came Oswald's voice from under the armchair at the other end of the large drawing room. His fat legs were sticking out. Mother and Father went off arm in arm to find him. And while they pretended not to see him and looked under every table and chair except the right one, Freddie and Katharine stuffed their pockets with seedcakes. Katharine emptied the bottom layer of the box of chocolate creams into a purse she had brought for this purpose. They would taste better up in the secret room.

That night Katharine and Freddie slipped out the back door into the cool night air. They ran across the wet grass in their bare feet, picked up the shelves, and hurried back into the house. The clock on the second-floor landing, ticking noisily, said quarter after two. Freddie stopped at Father's library. He took a small, rolled Oriental rug out of the closet and tucked it under his arm.

"What's that for?" whispered Katharine.

"Hush."

He disappeared into the drawing room and came out with embroidered blue pillows. He gave them to Katharine to carry.

"Oh, Freddie, that's stealing," gasped Katharine.

"Hush."

On the third floor, Katharine took her best petticoat and a tin of sweets they had collected. Then, stumbling along with the shelves and everything else, they headed up to the attic. When they were safe in the secret room, they unrolled the red and blue Oriental rug. It made the secret room look like a real sitting room. They placed their new shelves near where Freddie sat. Then they seated themselves, leaning against the embroidered blue pillows.

"Oh, Freddie, we can't steal," said Katharine.

"It's not stealing," said Freddie. "We're not taking anything out of the house. We're just *borrowing* the rug and pillows."

"I don't think Father and Mother will see it that way," said Katharine.

Freddie dug into his nightshirt pocket and took out scissors and a needle and thread from Mother's sewing basket. "She won't need them," he said. "She doesn't sew anymore."

Katharine's hand shook as she cut her best petticoat in two. She wondered if it would be missed. Freddie handed her a long branch he had cut from the hedges at the end of the garden. It was the curtain rod. Katharine held the waist of her petticoat around the wooden rod and sewed big, wiggly stitches. Meanwhile, Freddie laid some sweets on the table and stored the remainder neatly on the new shelves. He was tidier than he ever was downstairs.

He put both elbows on the table as he ate a piece of fruitcake. "*This* is the proper manners for this room."

Katharine ate a chocolate, smacking her lips. She licked every finger.

"That is *raw*-ther disgusting," said Freddie. With each word crumbs flew out of his mouth.

"That's ill-bred," said Katharine. "You are *not* a gentleman. Now would you like to see what I'm eating?" She opened her mouth wide, and chocolate dribbled out. And it continued to drip because she was laughing so hard. Freddie was laughing, too. Suddenly they stopped. They were making too much noise.

"If Miss Pritt could see us now," whispered Katharine.

"You know what we're doing?" said Freddie. "We're running away from home without really running away." Katharine forgot about being quiet and clapped her hands. Freddie said, "We'll have to borrow a lot more things to make this *really* a comfortable home."

Katharine nodded. Mother and Father might consider it stealing, but then they were too busy to think about Katharine and Freddie. Father had his law, and Mother had her parties. Now she and Freddie had their secret room.

·6·

IT WAS RAINING. The gray world of New York looked grayer still under the sheets of rain. Katharine was at the nursery table, staring out the window instead of at a long list of spelling words. She missed Mother. In the two and a half weeks that Miss Pritt had been with them, Katharine had not become used to Mother's being away. Mother had said, "I need to allow Miss Pritt to get her routine established. You mustn't fuss, Katharine. You see a lot of me." But when Katharine wanted her, Mother wasn't there. Like *now*. Mother always thought of wonderful things to do on rainy days.

"Your spelling words are so easy," said Freddie. He was in a bad mood, too. He kept kicking Katharine under the table, supposedly by mistake.

Lottie came in to pick up the breakfast dishes, piled on a tray in the corner. Miss Pritt looked in from her hallway. "You're late," she said.

"Oh, only because there's a regular ruckus downstairs. Mr. Sloat has discovered that some of the best silver is missing. And the Wedgwood plates—the white ones with pink roses that are antique and very rare. He is accusing all of us."

"Humph. I'm not surprised. He is a petty little man."

Freddie went pale. He pressed his foot on Katharine's. She kicked him.

Miss Pritt drew herself up to her full height and scowled down at Lottie. "Of course, this has nothing to do with me," she said. "Still, I'll go down and see what it's about." She took Oswald's hand and marched out of the nursery.

"I told you," whispered Katharine.

But Freddie had recovered. "Fiddlesticks," he said. "No one has asked us anything. Everything is well hidden, isn't it?" Katharine had to agree. "So don't worry. Let's go down the back stairs and listen."

They stood on the stairs next to the open pantry door. Everyone was shouting at once.

"This never happened when Mr. Harry was alive," shouted Mr. Sloat. "It must be someone *new* in the staff."

"Are you calling me a thief?" cried a new day maid.

"You called me one!" said a laundress.

Over the din came Miss Pritt's voice. "Mr. Sloat, I do not appreciate being included in your suspicions. I may be new, but Mrs. Outwater knows my references from some of the great houses of New York."

"I want an apology," cried Lottie. "Madam, the whole lot blamed me when the blue porcelain vase disappeared from the drawing room. They say I broke it and hid the pieces. Madam, it was the *thief* that took it."

"Please be calm," said Mother. "Stop accusing one another. We don't even know exactly what's missing. Let's take everything off the shelves and take count. I must admit things have been disappearing. Some pink pillows from my room. . . . It is very mysterious."

Miss Pritt said, "I'd like to know just what is missing. This is the first I've heard of it."

Freddie grinned. "She's so curious. She's going to stay in the pantry and stick her nose in everyone's business. We've got time on our hands." He winked at Katharine and ran up the stairs. Katharine followed. She was afraid to be left alone. What if someone accused her?

Freddie opened the window in the secret room, letting in the gray daylight. Then he put a jam tart on a plate and ate it with the very silver fork they were fighting about downstairs. "Sit down, Katharine."

"Well, I'll stay a minute," she said. She couldn't bring herself to lean against the pink satin cushions she had taken from Mother's dressing room.

Freddie was in great spirits. "I hope Miss Pritt is the number-one suspect." He licked his plate clean. It was the very white plate with hand-painted roses that Lottie said was so rare.

"Who would have thought those old white plates are so valuable?" cried Katharine. "Oh, dear!" Her eyes swept the room, which had been transformed in the past two weeks. There were nothing but stolen goods in it, including some of Father's motoring magazines on the table and the blue porcelain vase Lottie had been accused of smashing, filled with McSweeney's precious roses. Mother's pen and inkwell, her playing cards, and Father's checkers set from his closet were there, along with marbles and a few puzzles from the nursery. Games were more fun up in the secret room.

As for the shelves, they were crowded with goodies: sweets and cookies and cakes and chocolates and bottles of apple juice and orange juice; Freddie's Wild West books; and the plates and silverware, the remainder of which were being counted downstairs. Soon it would probably be discovered that three crystal glasses were missing, too. Katharine sighed.

"It's a shame you borrowed the best silverware and plates," said Freddie.

"I know. I just took the first things I saw." Katharine groaned as she remembered. Freddie called it their most daring adventure, done in the daytime because at night a maid slept on a cot in the pantry.

First Katharine had found her doll in a dusty corner of her closet and wrapped it in a blanket with a sack hidden underneath. Then she sneaked into the pantry while Freddie kept Eloise busy by pretending he wanted to learn French.

"How do you say 'cake'?" he asked.

"Gâteau," said Eloise.

"Gatto," said Freddie. "How do you say 'very good'?"

"Très bon."

"Tray bon," said Freddie.

"Non, non! Trrrrrrès bon," said Eloise, rolling her *r*'s.

Freddie rolled his. "Trrrrrray bon, your gatto. Can I have some?"

"Oui. Yes! You are adorrrable," said Eloise.

Meanwhile Katharine put her doll on the pantry counter and filled the sack under the blanket with whatever she could get her hands on. She had taken more than two of everything, because of the difficulty of washing up in the middle of the night. She was in too much of a panic to count, which was why they ended up with eight silver forks but only three spoons and four knives, three crystal glasses, and eight small plates.

She met Miss Pritt on the stairs.

"I'm taking my doll for a walk," said Katharine. The glass and china clinked under the blanket.

"Humph," snorted Miss Pritt. "This is the first time I've seen you play a proper girl's game. Where is Frederick?"

He was being hugged by Eloise, who ever since had called him her "adorrrable boy" and given him cookies. She ignored Katharine. They had laughed about this adventure, but now the whole house was in an uproar.

"I never thought there would be such a fuss over a few knives and forks," exclaimed Katharine. "Luckily, we don't need to borrow anything else."

"That's right," said Freddie. "I agree. We won't borrow anything else—except food, of course."

"I think we should return the plates tonight," said Katharine.

"No! That would be too suspicious." Then Freddie grinned. "Katharine, I think this is a good time for a game of checkers."

"It couldn't be a worse time," said Katharine.

"That's what makes it so daring. We must see who is the champion." Freddie set up the checkers set. They had played ten games of checkers so far and were tied five to five. Checkers could be dull downstairs; but up in the secret room where they shouldn't be, playing it was very exciting. Katharine had made a great effort to tie the score.

They had enjoyed many games in the secret room during the past two weeks—marbles on the soft Oriental rug, card games with Mother's cards. All of the scores were recorded in Katharine's diary, which now hung by a string on a nail in the wall. She had removed it from her room, afraid that Miss Pritt would read it.

"I'll begin," said Freddie, calmly moving his black checker. Katharine moved her red piece, but soon Freddie jumped his black piece over three of hers.

"I refuse to play!" cried Katharine. "I can't concentrate with all the trouble downstairs. They may be looking for us right now." She swept her hand across the board, scattering all the pieces.

Freddie threw a pillow at her. But he followed her when she banged her way out of the room. Soon they were sitting, a little out of breath, in their seats at the nursery table, their spelling lists in their hands. Moments later, Katharine heard Mother's and Miss Pritt's voices in the hall.

"We can surely live without a few spoons and forks,"

Mother was saying. "Now, Miss Pritt, don't be upset. No one is blaming you."

They entered the nursery. Oswald was in Mother's arms.

"There you are—I've missed you so," said Mother. "Why, look at the nursery. Neat as a pin! It's in perfect order since you took over, Miss Pritt."

Miss Pritt stopped huffing. "The children are in better order, too, madam," she said, looking thoroughly pleased with herself. "As you can see, while I've been out of the nursery, they have been quietly studying their spelling."

"They look like little angels," said Mother, patting Katharine's and Freddie's heads.

Why, Katharine thought, Freddie's right. There's nothing to be afraid of—*we've outsmarted them all.*

·7·

MOTHER SAID, "The children deserve a reward. It's a rainy day, and they have been so good, staying inside without complaining and studying their spelling. We will dine out tonight. I will telegraph Mr. Outwater to change clothes at his club and join us at the Waldorf-Astoria Hotel."

Miss Pritt frowned. "Pardon me, madam, but I don't believe that will be good for the children. It will upset their schedule. They will be up late, and they need their sleep."

Mother's excited smile faded. "Oh, Miss Pritt. They need an outing after being in the house all day."

Miss Pritt's mouth was pursed. "Madam, I have just gotten Katharine and Frederick *off* sweets, and I'm sure at the Waldorf they will stuff themselves with sugary desserts. Also, they do yawn during the day, and sometimes sleep at their nap time."

"Well, this once, we'll take them. I will hire a large brougham carriage to drive us there early—say, six. Children, you are going to see the largest hotel in the world. One thousand rooms! And you may ride the elevators. Miss Pritt, you will come, too. You have been so good to give up your day off for two weeks in order to get the children settled. You will come, and then we will be able to bring Oswald. We'll have a lovely time!"

Mother and Miss Pritt then retired for one of their endless talks.

"I wish Miss Pritt would take her days off," whispered Katharine. "Isn't she a mean thing not wanting us to go to the Waldorf?"

As it turned out, going to the Waldorf was not like going places with Mother and Father in the country. Miss Pritt said, "All of New York society will be there. You must bathe and wear your new clothes. Katharine, I will comb your hair."

"*This* will be a test of your manners," Miss Pritt said grimly, as they waited in the front hall for Mother. Katharine was in an uncomfortable white dress with huge balloon sleeves, and Freddie wore a suit and a shirt with a very stiff collar and cuffs. At last Mother came down looking beautiful in a blue silk gown. Ropes of pearls hung from her neck.

It was still raining. They drove down Fifth Avenue to Thirty-fourth Street and turned into the Waldorf's covered carriage drive. Lines of hansom cabs were parked outside.

"Here we are," said Mother. "You will love it, children! It's very grand."

An imposing doorman opened the carriage door.

Other uniformed men took Katharine's jacket and Mother's cape when they went inside.

While Mother was greeted by a friend, Katharine looked around her. She was standing in a long corridor with gold ornamentation on the walls and ceiling. People jammed the passage, and Katharine was surprised to see that everyone was staring at her. She checked her skirt—was her petticoat hanging down, unbuttoned? Had her stocking gotten loose from its garter?

She caught sight of Father at the end of the hall and ran to him. He was dressed in his evening clothes, with pearl buttons down his white shirtfront. "I'm proud of my family," he said. They watched Mother come to them. She was so beautiful that she attracted many admiring glances. Father explained to Katharine and Freddie, "This is the famous Peacock Alley. It's named that because people strut here, just as peacocks do, showing off their jewels and clothes. All of New York society passes through, and the stars of the theater."

There were several dining rooms and cafés, but Father and Mother wanted to take them to the Palm Room. "We have not reserved," said Father. "I shouldn't think there's a table to be had. But we'll try." A long line of people waited to enter the Palm Room. They were stopped by a red velvet rope behind which stood a stout man who was greeting some people by name and ignoring others.

Father said, "Come along. We'll talk to Oscar."

Mother whispered, "Children, Oscar is one of the most powerful men in New York. He decides who will be seated and who will not."

Father walked to the front of the line. "Good evening, Oscar," he said. "We've brought the family and we're hoping to dine."

Oscar bowed low to them. "Good evening, Mr. Outwater, Mrs. Outwater. So very pleased to see you. Of course we have a table for you and the children. Come this way."

He led them to a table. In the center was a candelabrum with little red lampshades. Waiters in white shirts gathered around them. One waiter pulled out a gold chair for Katharine. She had chosen a seat next to Father and as far away from Miss Pritt as possible. Two cushions were brought for Oswald's seat between Mother and Miss Pritt.

Mother and Father were nodding at people at other tables and seemed very happy, especially with Oscar's attention. "It is a sign that we have been accepted in New York," said Father.

A menu was put in front of Katharine. Everything was written in French. As Father translated for her, she knew she didn't want lamb with mashed chestnuts; she didn't want some sweet little frogs' legs; she didn't want clammy oysters; and she didn't want diamond-back terrapin, which turned out to be turtle.

Oscar said, "We have canvasback duck tonight, stuffed with foie gras. Mmm!" He kissed his fingers.

"I'll have it," said Katharine, remembering Mrs. Hodkins's delicious duck stew.

"You will not regret it," said Oscar.

"Well, children," said Father after they had ordered and Oscar had gone. "Did you have a nice day?"

They nodded. Katharine did not feel free to talk with Miss Pritt sitting so stiffly across from her.

"How is the puzzle coming?" asked Father.

"The sky is half done," said Freddie.

"Good, good." Father smiled at Miss Pritt. Then there was a silence.

"I am going to have a surprise for you soon," said Father.

"A puppy!" exclaimed Katharine, leaning over and sending a fork flying to the floor.

A watchful waiter pounced on it and gave Katharine another one.

"No, not a puppy," said Father. "You will find out on June nineteenth. It's a surprise, so don't ask any questions."

More silence. Were Mother and Father feeling awkward, too, with Miss Pritt there?

At last they were surrounded by waiters. A crisp, dark brown piece of meat was placed in front of Katharine. The meat was tough. She tried the stuffing and quickly spit it into her napkin. It was liver. She hoped no one would notice that she was not eating, but Miss Pritt had her eagle eye on their plates. "Katharine," she whispered, pointing to her food.

"Oh, dear," said Mother. "You don't like your duck. Why did we let you order such a thing?"

"Madam, she should eat it," said Miss Pritt.

Oscar returned. "And how is the duck, Miss Outwater? You have not touched it. Have we done something wrong?"

"Well, the stuffing . . ."

70

"It is not to your taste?" asked Oscar. His eye caught the waiter's. "Take it away," he said, waving his hand at the dish. "Tell the chef to prepare duck à l'orange."

Katharine's plate was taken away, and another dark, hard duck wing and breast arrived, this time in a bitter orange sauce. With all the thank-yous of Mother and Father to Oscar, it was clear to Katharine that she would have to eat it. Miss Pritt was glowering at her across the table.

Just then Father swooped down on the duck with his fork and knife and removed it to his own plate. "Katharine, you are always so good about sharing," he said with a twinkle in his eye.

Everyone laughed. But then they stopped, because Miss Pritt was not laughing. Oh, she put such a damper on things!

Father gave Katharine some of his steak and vegetables. After a while, the waiters started swarming around their table, clearing it. It was time for dessert.

Freddie knew what he wanted on the menu. He had seen the waiters set a dessert on fire. "Here it is," he said. "Baked Alaska flambé."

"Splendid," said Mother. "It will arrive on your plate in flames!"

Then Katharine would have nothing less. She searched for more "flambé."

"I know just the thing," said Mother, pointing to her menu. "Here, Katharine. Chocolate cake flambé. That will make for a nice little fire." Mother clapped her hands and laughed.

The look on Miss Pritt's face said that someone who

had not finished her main course had no right to dessert.

Oswald was becoming restless. He tried to wriggle out of his seat and was stopped by Miss Pritt. "Mama," he whined. Father's coffee arrived, and while Father stood up to greet a party of people passing by, Oswald grabbed a handful of sugar lumps and dropped them in the cup.

"Pardon me, sir," said a waiter. "Those lumps are wrapped in paper. Allow me to get you another coffee."

Katharine smothered a laugh. Miss Pritt scowled. "He's too young to be here, sir." Father nodded.

Then the dessert cart arrived. One waiter mixed an orange sauce in a pan and poured a dark liquid on it. "That's cognac," said Mother.

At the same time, the sauce for Katharine's chocolate cake was doused with cognac by another waiter. With a flourish, both waiters lit matches. *Whoosh.* The sauce went up in flames. Two feet of blue-orange flame rose from the pans.

Oswald shouted, "Fi-yah! Fi-yah!" He took his glass and threw water at the fire. He missed the flames, but he hit one of the waiters in the face. Suddenly Oswald was out of his chair and running through the Palm Room, yelling, *"Fi-yah!"*

All heads turned. Some people were laughing.

Miss Pritt was very quick. She caught Oswald between two tables, picked him up as he screamed, and left the restaurant. The last sight they had of him was of fat, kicking legs.

Mother was blushing; all eyes in the Palm Room

72

were on them. "We'll let Miss Pritt handle Oswald," she said. "She is so capable." She turned to the waiter who had received Oswald's fire-prevention efforts in the face. "I'm so *very* sorry." He nodded and wiped his face with a napkin.

Service began again in the Palm Room. Katharine's sauce, now with small, curling blue flames, was poured on her cake and put in front of her. She stared, fascinated, a smile on her lips. Oswald was still the best distraction for Miss Pritt! All her tension had left along with Miss Pritt. Katharine discovered she was starving. She noticed that everything in the room was sparkling—the jewels, the lights. She heard soft music being played, and found a trio of musicians hidden behind some palm plants. She was enjoying the chocolate cake.

Freddie, who had been silent most of the evening, was suddenly talking. "Oswald wants to be a fireman," he said. "He—"

But Father interrupted him. "It wasn't the wisest plan to bring Oswald here," he said to Mother.

"I am so embarrassed," admitted Mother. She got up to see how Oswald and Miss Pritt were, and returned quickly. "Oswald is sitting quietly. I told Miss Pritt to go home, but she insists on staying so that she can take Katharine and Freddie, too. She is aware that we want to greet friends, and it is long past the children's bedtime. Really, Miss Pritt is so devoted."

"Oh, Mother! Father!" said Freddie, red in the face.

Katharine just stared at her chocolate cake. She had lost her appetite again.

· 8 ·

A T LAST, three weeks after she had come, it was finally Miss Pritt's day off. Katharine could hardly hide her joy when she saw Miss Pritt put on her black jacket.

"I hope you have a lovely time with your aunt," said Mother.

"Oswald woke early," said Miss Pritt. "He should have an early nap." She was buttoning her gloves.

"Don't worry," said Mother. "We'll make sure he doesn't get overtired."

Now Miss Pritt was putting on her black hat. Hurry, thought Katharine, hurry!

Then they were saying good-bye, and the rustle of Miss Pritt's skirts faded down the hall. Freddie and Katharine and Oswald jumped into Mother's arms. "Oh, darlings, I've a wonderful surprise for you," she said. "I'm taking you to Long Island, to the beach."

"The beach!"

"Hurrah!"

"After all, it's June, and hot enough for swimming,"

said Mother. "We're invited to use the cottage of some friends by the bay. You've only swum in a lake. You're going to love the bay! And there's another surprise."

Mother brought out navy flannel swimming trunks and shirts for the boys from a bag, and a navy woolen swimming dress, stockings, and bloomers for Katharine.

"Is that the surprise?" asked Katharine, disappointed.

"No. I suggest you go downstairs. Remember, Father said there would be a surprise on June nineteenth."

They raced down the stairs and bumped into Father in the front hall.

"It's about time," he said. "Our carriage awaits us." He offered Katharine his arm, and they walked outside.

"Oh, Father! You mean a *horseless* carriage," gasped Katharine.

Parked in front of the house was a shiny black automobile with gleaming brass headlights and trim.

"Father, why is a Benz here?" demanded Freddie.

"For the simple reason that it belongs to us," said Father happily.

"Oh, take us for a ride!"

"Please, Father!"

"Yes, yes, just as soon as Mother and Oswald come down." Father patted the fender. "It's designed by a German engineer named Karl Benz. There are only a handful in America."

"I know! The Benz wins a lot of the races in Europe," said Freddie, who had read father's motoring magazines up in the secret room. He examined the front. "Is it a two- or four-cylinder engine?"

"Four," said Father, rocking on his heels and looking proud. "It will go up to forty-five miles per hour. But wait a minute, Freddie. You sound very informed. Will you kindly return my *Automobile Topics*? I'd like to read it, too."

Freddie laughed, and he and Katharine leaped up the high step to the backseat. It smelled of new leather. Freddie leaned over the front seat and squeezed the rubber bulb of the horn. *Honk!*

"Don't touch," said a young man in a leather cap and suit. "And please, no feet on the seats."

"Children, this is Gifford," said Father. "He's our chauffeur. He's in charge of the Benz."

"Why aren't you in charge?" asked Katharine. Gifford seemed unfriendly.

"I can't be in charge when I'm working at the office," Father answered.

Mother appeared, looking strange in a motoring costume: a long gray duster over her dress, goggles, and a motoring hat with yards of veiling tied under her chin. "I'm ready," she said. "Gifford, we put our lives in your hands."

"Don't be silly," said Father. "You won't find a more perfect engine in the world."

Mother sat in the back with Katharine and Freddie. She put a bundle on the floor by her feet. Father held Oswald in his lap in the front.

"Gifford, we'll go first to the office," he said. "Then

you will drive Mrs. Outwater wherever she wishes. What have you planned, Diana?"

"Oh, something outside the city," she said vaguely, and lifted her goggles to wink at Katharine and Freddie.

"Excellent," said Father. "An opportunity for this machine to run on a highway."

Gifford pulled his goggles over his eyes and pushed a switch at the controls. He ran to the front to crank the engine. Gifford turned a rod around and around, and then—*bang!*—there was an explosion. The Benz started chugging noisily and shaking. Katharine and Mother gripped the seat, but Freddie just shouted, "It's started!" Gifford slid quickly behind the wheel and moved a lever. The Benz lurched forward.

"Hurrah," cheered Freddie.

"Oh, mercy!" cried Mother. She held on more tightly. They were off down Madison Avenue.

Men walking to work looked up at the sound of the motorcar. Everyone gaped at it, for there were very few automobiles on the streets of New York. A horse even became frightened and reared.

In the meantime, Katharine had decided that a motorcar was not frightening at all. It was splendid! The buildings looked like a blur as the Outwaters sped along. They passed another motorcar—a little machine, not a grand touring car like theirs. Freddie and Katharine cheered and waved. "Faster!" shouted Katharine.

Father turned around. "Twelve miles per hour is the city speed limit."

"Slower," said Mother.

She needn't have worried. The streets were full of carriages, trucks, wagons, omnibuses, and pushcarts. There was no chance to go faster, especially downtown where the streets became narrow and the buildings were towers that reached to the heavens. Gifford stopped on Wall Street in front of Father's office. A crowd gathered around them—men in bowler hats and dark suits, just like Father. Father looked very proud.

"Have a nice time," he said, getting out. "Diana, darling, shouldn't you have brought Lottie with you?"

"Nonsense," said Mother. "Have you forgotten how I managed in the country all by myself?" Father nodded and waved good-bye, and Mother moved to the front seat with Oswald. She handed Gifford a map marked with the route to the bay.

Gifford frowned. "I hope the roads aren't muddy or sandy. This is not a horse."

Mother gave Gifford a stern look. "This route is proposed by an automobile magazine."

Again they were off, leaving the city and its clouds of black smoke for the flat countryside of Long Island. They passed fields and woods and saw little villages in the distance. The Benz gathered speed on the gravel highway, and the wind whipped Katharine's hair against her cheeks. She leaned back against the smooth leather seat, feeling very happy. They had gotten rid of Miss Pritt, and they were driving to the beach in their new automobile.

Soon they turned onto a dirt road. The Benz bumped over stones and in and out of deep ruts, stirring up a cloud of dust. They passed a huge white mansion with closed shutters.

Mother laughed. "This is what my friends call their 'country cottage.' It must have sixty rooms! The house is closed. But further on is a house for the servants, which is open. Drive on, Gifford."

They stopped by a small white house. "Oh, children, look at the water!" exclaimed Mother. Katharine stood on the seat. Beyond the house was the beach, and the bay, gray-blue with whitecaps.

"Thank goodness, we made it," said Mother while Gifford opened the door.

"There's nothing to worry about with this machine," sniffed Gifford. "But the road isn't fit for a Benz, madam." The once-shiny radiator was covered with dust.

Nobody listened. Mother was talking to a servant at the cottage, and Katharine and Freddie disappeared inside to put on their bathing clothes.

It was as if Miss Pritt had never existed. They ate delicious goodies from Mother's picnic basket whenever they wished; they swam in the cold bay despite their blue lips and chattering teeth. Mother used her parasol to protect herself from the sun, and only went into the water up to her knees.

"Isn't this nicer than the muddy old lake with its mucky bottom?" said Mother.

"Yes," said Katharine. It happened to be true, but Mother looked so anxious that Katharine would have said yes just to please her. Mother wrapped a towel around Katharine. She sat very still and enjoyed

Mother's softness and warmth, while Oswald played with his pail nearby.

Freddie came running with something in his hands. "Look, Mother. Starfish!"

"They're just beautiful," said Mother. "Perfect little stars. I've never seen them before. It's rare to find them on the beach."

This made Freddie and Katharine decide to collect them. They gathered a dozen; next they collected transparent orange shells and yellow ones, hard little white shells and ribbed black ones, and handfuls of pretty colored stones. They brought all these treasures back to New York in the picnic basket and dumped them on the floor of the nursery. The shells were washed in a basin of water; then holes were hammered in them. Katharine and Freddie threaded yarn through the holes and made necklaces for Mother, which they tied around her neck. Katharine was hammering more holes in shells when they heard "Goodness!" from the doorway. The hammer fell out of Katharine's hand, she was so surprised to see the black figure standing there.

"Goodness!" repeated Miss Pritt.

"Why, Miss Pritt, you're back early," said Mother. "Didn't you visit your aunt?"

"I have seen my aunt," said Miss Pritt. "I never take a very long day off." She looked shocked by the sand, seaweed, and broken shells scattered all over the floor.

"I'm sorry for the disorder," said Mother, standing up. "I'll have Lottie sweep. We went to the bay for a swim."

"A swim—at this time of the year? Wasn't the water too cold?" Miss Pritt looked as if she were making a great effort to control her temper. She unbuttoned her gloves.

"You seem to have brought half the beach back with you," said a deep voice. Father!

"Indeed we did," said Mother, laughing now that Father was here. "Look at my lovely necklaces, and those starfish. Isn't it rare to find them on the beach?"

"Oho! I've never seen a starfish before. Very interesting," he said. "How was your ride?"

"Perfect," said Freddie, "but we need goggles."

"You shall have them," said Father. "Well, I'm glad to see Miss Pritt is back." He turned to Mother. "Diana, we've been invited to dinner. It's rather sudden, but important." He took Mother's arm. "The children will be safe and sound with Miss Pritt. You just have time to dress. Children, we'll return later to say good-night. Come, Diana."

Miss Pritt said, "Glad to be of service." Then, as soon as Mother and Father were gone, she took a broom and angrily swept everything into the wastebasket.

"Don't touch those starfish!" exclaimed Katharine. She got on her hands and knees and gathered them to her pinafore. Tears were in her eyes.

"Take them to your room if you insist on keeping them," said Miss Pritt.

Katharine laid the starfish on top of her bookshelves. She thought they would make a lovely decoration for the walls of the secret room. Except for some stones, they were the only things left from their outing with

Mother. But by bedtime the starfish had begun to smell. They stank.

"It's impossible. You cannot keep them," said Miss Pritt. Just then Mother and Father came to say good-night.

"Mother," cried Katharine. "Miss Pritt wants to throw away our starfish!"

"Madam, they smell, and it's only going to get worse as they dry out," said Miss Pritt.

Mother poked her head into Katharine's room and sniffed. She was in a hurry. "I don't smell anything," she said. "Perhaps I am wearing too much perfume. Miss Pritt, please save some of the starfish—they can dry out in a closet."

"She'll throw them away," wailed Katharine. She was crying, but whether it was over the starfish or over Miss Pritt being back and Mother and Father going out again, she didn't know.

"Now, Katharine, you're just tired," said Mother. "We did have a lovely day." She blew Katharine a kiss, because she had to be careful of her pompadour. She left her purse and her feathered boa on Katharine's chest of drawers and followed Father to Freddie's room.

Katharine stopped crying. Mother had told Miss Pritt to save some of the starfish. Katharine would make sure that happened.

· 9 ·

"I SHOULD LIKE to talk to Katharine and Freddie alone," said Mother the next morning, without her usual smile.

"Very well, madam," said Miss Pritt.

Mother marched them to her bedroom and had them sit down on a pink sofa. Katharine sat on the edge, fidgeting. Mother could look this angry only about the secret room. She must have found them out. Katharine nudged Freddie, who gave her a worried look.

"Why are you looking at each other?" asked Mother. "Do you have something to confess?"

Silence. Mother frowned. "My, you two look guilty," she said. "Last night I went to an elegant dinner party given by Mr. and Mrs. Pospinwall. Now listen carefully to what happened." The name "Pospinwall" seemed familiar to Katharine, but she didn't understand why Mother wanted to talk about a dinner party.

Mother continued her story. It was during the fourth course of dinner, which was a roast and looked quite fresh, that a strange odor of something rotting spread through the dining room. Mother noticed that Mrs. Pospinwall, who usually had her nose turned up haughtily, was wiggling it instead. Sniffing. As the fifth course of salad and cheese was served, Mrs. Pospinwall started to look distressed. Was it a particularly smelly cheese that was making the dining room smell so? Two men were sitting with their fingers under their noses.

It must be a smelly cheese, Mother decided. But the strawberry soufflé was also smothered by the foul odor, which could very well have been due to rotten eggs. What were rotten eggs doing in Mrs. Pospinwall's soufflé?

Strangely enough, the smell traveled with the ladies up to Mrs. Pospinwall's chambers after dinner. Mother followed the tall, gray-haired Mrs. Pospinwall upstairs. First she took great offense when she realized that Mrs. Pospinwall was sniffing around her; then Mother decided not to be offended. She even sat down next to Mrs. Pospinwall when they returned to the drawing room.

"What lovely flowers," said Mother.

"I'm especially fond of their delicate scent," said Mrs. Pospinwall. It was an unfortunate choice of subject because all anyone could smell in the drawing room was rotting fish.

"How are the children?" asked Mrs. Pospinwall.

"They are well, and very good," said Mother. She sneezed, and opened her purse to get her handkerchief. "The children didn't like moving to town, but—*oh!*" Inside her purse were three starfish. She snapped the purse shut, but a horrible odor had already shot out. She was sure Mrs. Pospinwall had noticed. Her purse was silver mesh, a material with tiny holes, and it was through these holes that the smell was seeping out.

"What was I saying?" asked Mother. "Something about the children . . ."

"What was it that surprised you just then?" asked Mrs. Pospinwall, staring at Mother's purse.

"Nothing. I forgot to bring a hankie."

"I don't see why that should shock you," said Mrs. Pospinwall.

"You asked about the children," said Mother. "They are very naughty."

"But you just told me they are good."

"I've never heard you call the children naughty," said Father, who had just returned with the other men from smoking a cigar in Mr. Pospinwall's study.

"And sick," said Mother. "They all have colds. I do believe we should go home."

"But don't you have our treasure of a nurse, Miss Pritt?" asked Mrs. Pospinwall, studying Mother keenly. "Nurses know so much more than we mothers."

"The children are as well as can be," said Father. "Weren't they all shouting for you at the top of their lungs just before we went out tonight?"

Mr. Pospinwall sat down in an armchair next to Mother. "We're delighted you've made New York your home," he said. He seemed willing to put up with the smell near Mother.

Mother managed to smile, and Mr. Pospinwall, who was small and pixieish, smiled back.

"You are a beautiful addition to our drab town," he said, and his eyes shot over to the imposing figure of Mrs. Pospinwall to see if she had heard. She most likely had, because she was frowning at him.

"It's wonderful to be here," said Mother. "But now I really m-must get back to my sick children." Mother stood up and made Father leave.

During the ride home she dropped the starfish over the side of the Benz. Then she explained to Father that she had felt sick, probably because of the terrible smell in Mrs. Pospinwall's house. Father agreed it had been beastly.

"There must have been a dead rat in the walls," he said.

"I thought it wise not to tell Father the truth," said Mother to Katharine and Freddie. Katharine was sitting on her clammy hands. "You know," added Mother, "the law firm that Father wants to join is Mr. Pospinwall's firm. It's called Pospinwall, Butler, and Gates. It all depends on the Pospinwalls, so you can see how important they are to Father. Now, out with it—who is the culprit?"

"I just wanted to save a few," Katharine whispered, gazing down at her lap. She added, "You left your purse in my room, and you told Miss Pritt to put a few starfish aside, and I knew she wouldn't do it." She looked up at Mother. "And I was right. As soon as you left, she threw them all into the wastebasket and took it away so I couldn't rescue them."

"Oh, Katharine," said Mother, shaking her head.

"It was the worst hiding place in the world," cried Freddie.

"I had to think fast," said Katharine.

"You didn't think at all!" said Mother.

"I'm sorry," whispered Katharine. She really was. She hadn't wanted to ruin anything for Mother and Father.

"Come here." Mother's arms were outstretched, and Katharine rushed into them. She felt Freddie patting her back. He looked happy. The secret room had not been discovered.

"I forgive you this time, darling," said Mother. "But we must all help Father." Katharine heard a note of worry in Mother's voice.

"There was a comical side to it," said Mother, suddenly laughing a bit. "Mrs. Pospinwall talking about the delicate odor of her flowers while the whole room smelled like a fish shop!" They all laughed. But Katharine had realized something during Mother's story, and it spoiled her relief now. The Pospinwalls had given Miss Pritt to them. Father wanted to join Mr. Pospinwall's firm, so he would never make the Pospinwalls angry by sending Miss Pritt away. She was here to stay.

·10·

MOTHER and Father were going to Boston. Father had business there, and he said, "Mother deserves a little holiday now that we have Miss Pritt. It's only for four days." It seemed like a long time to Katharine. The most Mother had ever been away before was for one night.

Gifford was placing the valises in the Benz and was ready to drive Mother and Father to the railroad station.

"I shall miss you so," said Mother. "I'll bring you presents." Then she turned to Miss Pritt. "Please plan some special outings for the children. Oh, I hope they'll be all right."

Miss Pritt smiled in her sugary way. "There is nothing to worry about, madam."

"Of course we're not worried," said Father to Miss Pritt. After one last kiss to each child, he and Mother got into the Benz and Gifford drove them away. They threw kisses until they were out of sight.

Katharine stood on the sidewalk, feeling alone and unprotected. How could Mother and Father leave!

She felt a prodding at her back. "Come along," said Miss Pritt. "It's time for the park. We are going to the lake."

This was Miss Pritt's idea of a special outing—to take them to a different part of Central Park. They had been just once to the Menagerie with her, and had had two short visits to the carousel. Freddie had decided Miss Pritt liked to meet the other nurses near Sixty-ninth Street, where they had gone the first day she arrived. She found every excuse possible to avoid doing anything else.

Today Miss Pritt took them down a long, tree-lined mall to the lake, where Miss Victory and Amelia Whittaker were waiting. Albert Fitzhugh, a boy Freddie's age, was also there with his nurse and baby sister. The nurses sat down on a bench near the great stone fountain by the edge of the lake. Across was a boathouse where rowboats could be rented.

"Katharine and I want to take out a rowboat," said Freddie.

"No," said Miss Pritt. She offered them instead a ride in a motorized swan boat, but neither Freddie nor Katharine wanted to go.

"Birdie," cried Oswald, pointing to the swan boat. Miss Pritt took him for a ride, leaving Katharine and Freddie in the care of the other nurses. Freddie went off to play ball, but Katharine didn't care to. Albert Fitzhugh had already seated himself on a bench and was reading. He was a nice boy but had no interest in sports and preferred his books. This made Katharine and Freddie more worried about school. They were going to be dunces, just as Miss Pritt had said.

Katharine walked by the edge of the lake, her hands clasped behind her back, her head bent. She couldn't share with Freddie how sad she felt. He would call her a baby for missing her mama and papa.

Suddenly a little frog, hardly an inch long, jumped near her boot. She hadn't seen a frog since the country. She watched it take huge flying leaps, practically a foot high. It kept hopping in circles.

"I think it's lost," said Katharine to herself. "Poor little frog." She caught it and peeked between her fingers. It was a sweet little baby, just changed from a tadpole. Then she had an idea. She ran to Freddie. "Freddie, come and see what I found!"

He threw the ball to some shabby-looking boys and looked into her cupped hands. "He's tiny," Freddie exclaimed.

"What makes you sure it's a *he*?" said Katharine. "I just know it's a baby girl. She's lost—she's been jumping in circles. She probably can't find her parents, and she'll die unless . . . I take her to the secret room and make her my pet."

"A splendid idea," Freddie said.

"Thank you." Katharine was thrilled to have thought of it. "We've got to get her home now," she said.

"I don't know how we're going to do that. We just got here," said Freddie. "Oh, look who's coming."

Amelia walked toward them carrying her large hoop and a stick. "What are you holding?" she asked.

"Nothing," said Katharine. She and Amelia did not get along any better now than on the first day they had met.

Amelia put down her hoop and tapped Katharine's hand. "Let me see."

"I don't have to," said Katharine, "and don't tell the nurses."

"Why? What have you got?" Amelia turned in the direction of Miss Victory.

Katharine had to do something to stop her, so she stuck out her boot and tripped her.

"Oh, you horrid thing," cried Amelia. She stood up. Her white stockings had green stains at the knees. She grabbed Katharine's hand and tried to pry open her fingers. Katharine was surprised how strong she was.

"Stop it, Amelia! Freddie, help me," cried Katharine. She was afraid the baby frog would be hurt in the scuffle.

Freddie put his arms around Amelia's waist and pulled her away.

"Miss Victoreeee!" screamed Amelia.

Miss Victory waddled across the grass and slapped Freddie's arms. "How dare you hold Amelia that way!"

Freddie let go. But once freed, Amelia gave Katharine a kick in the shin.

"I saw that," said a stern voice by the lake. Miss Pritt stepped off the boat with Oswald and hurried toward them. For once, she wasn't glaring at Katharine—her dark look was directed at Amelia. "I saw you kick Katharine," she said.

Katharine decided to moan and to rub her shin.

"Your two started it," said Miss Victory. "Two against one. How low!"

Amelia's and Katharine's screams had brought a group of people to watch—Albert Fitzhugh, his finger marking his page in his book; the boys in dirty clothes and their mother; an elegant lady on horseback.

Miss Pritt eyed the elegant lady, and more to her than anyone else said, "My children do not start fights. I resent the accusation."

The two nurses were arguing! Amelia plucked at Miss Victory's sleeve, trying to get her attention. Meanwhile, Katharine slipped the little frog into one of her pockets and stood with her hands in them.

Miss Pritt drew herself to her full height and said, "Come along, children. We are leaving." She shook off Amelia, who was now tapping her arm. She grabbed Freddie's ball out of a raggedy boy's hands without even a thank-you. Miss Pritt could be very rude. She glanced out of the corner of her eye at the elegant lady and then whisked them out of the park, wheeling Oswald's carriage at a furious pace.

"Amelia started it," said Katharine when they reached Fifth Avenue.

"I don't care for your explanations!" said Miss Pritt. "Ladies do not fight. And gentlemen *never* fight ladies, Frederick. I have been disgraced. You will stay in your rooms until supper. I hope Amelia's nurse has the sense to punish her. Frederick, how often have I told you *not* to play with children of an inferior social station? Did you see how unsanitary their clothing is? They must have germs."

Katharine sighed. For one second, it had seemed as if Miss Pritt were on their side. At least, she was on her way home with her little frog, just as quickly as she had wished.

She fussed over her new pet the rest of the day, giving it her pink hatbox in the closet. She sneaked down to the garden and got some moss, which she dampened and put inside the hatbox. Freddie escaped, too, and found food for the frog—black, squirming slugs that were living under some dead leaves behind the toolshed. Katharine took the frog to the bathroom twice for a swim in the tub.

Still, the afternoon passed slowly. Katharine thought bitterly of Mother's asking Miss Pritt to take them on some *special* outings. Mother didn't understand anything.

In the middle of the night, Freddie helped settle the frog in the secret room. By now the hatbox was a soggy mess. Freddie gave the frog the tin box that usually held his soldiers. He also stopped by Father's library, although they had agreed not to borrow anything else from the house. "This is a necessity," said Freddie. "We need something very heavy to hold water and not tip over." He took Father's marble ashtray from his desk. They also tiptoed to Mother's dressing room and ripped the veils off two hats in her closet—another necessity. The veils would be tied around the top of the tin box so that the frog could not jump out. "The hats look better without the veils," declared Freddie.

Then up to the secret room they went and set up the frog's new home. Freddie was such a help, Katharine thought. He didn't complain about having been punished, even though it had all been her fault.

"When you find a pet, I'll help you get it settled," Katharine said. "I *promise*. And I keep my promises, not like Mother."

"I don't think she ever means to get us a puppy," said Freddie.

"So we have to get our own pets. It's just what we would do if we still lived in the country!"

"Come on," said Freddie. "Stop kissing that frog. Let's go down."

Halfway down the stairs from the fourth to the third floor, they heard Miss Pritt calling. Her voice cut through the darkness. "Is someone there?"

Katharine and Freddie stood, frozen, in the middle of the stairs, gripping each other. They heard the sound of slippers shuffling, but in which direction it was impossible to tell. It was very black in the hall below. With Mother and Father gone, the lamp near their rooms was not lit. Again there was a sound. . . .

"She's going to our rooms!" gasped Freddie. "Come on. We'll pretend we went to the bathroom." He pulled Katharine down the stairs. They bumped into Miss Pritt in the dark hall. She looked very tall in a white nightgown with a high, ruffled neck that gleamed in the darkness.

"What are you doing out of bed?" she asked.

Freddie said, "K-Katharine was afraid to go to the bathroom alone."

"Humph. I thought there was a prowler in the house. Back to your rooms."

No more night visits, thought Katharine as she got into her cold bed. Until now, Miss Pritt had never awakened. Was it because Mother and Father were gone that she was more alert?

Katharine heard a creak outside. Miss Pritt must be lurking in the hall. She didn't trust them to stay in bed. No, they could not go up to the secret room at night—not until Mother and Father were back. She would have to find a way to feed her frog during the day.

"I think I'll call her Alice," she whispered to herself. Now if only Freddie could find a pet, too. . . .

·11·

TWO DAYS went by, and Freddie didn't find a pet. He had decided on a turtle, but none turned up in the park.

The fourth day of Mother and Father's Boston holiday was a Sunday, so there were no lessons. They were preparing to go out, dressed in their Sunday best, when a mouse ran across the nursery floor, right by Miss Pritt's black boot. She screamed.

Katharine shrugged. "It's only a little mouse. There were hundreds in our barn."

Freddie's face had lit up. "I'll catch it, Miss Pritt," he said.

The mouse was small. It hugged the wall and ran into the little hall, then on into Miss Pritt's bedroom. Freddie followed. There were thumps and bangs and the scraping sound of furniture being moved. Soon Freddie reappeared.

"I got him," he said. "I had to catch him with your quilt, Miss Pritt. I threw him out the window."

"Well done," said Miss Pritt. "Goodness knows what has happened to my room." She left to investigate.

Freddie's mouth curved into a happy smile, and he pointed to his knickers pocket. "I can't keep him in my room—I haven't anything big enough to put him in. He's a baby—so frisky! I've got to get him settled upstairs right now. You distract Miss Pritt."

"Wait, Freddie. What should I do?"

"Anything. Pretend you're sick."

"No! I don't want her to touch me."

Freddie was running down the hall. He stopped. "You *promised* to help." Then he disappeared upstairs.

Katharine wrung her hands. She wished she could think of some other way to distract Miss Pritt. She could hear her moving her furniture. Then Miss Pritt came in.

"Well, Katharine? Why are you standing in the middle of the room?"

"I . . . feel . . . s-sick," said Katharine. No sooner had she said it than she really did feel sick. Miss Pritt was hovering over her and feeling her forehead.

"It's my s-stomach," said Katharine, regretting that she had taken Freddie's suggestion. "I think I'm going to v-vomit."

Miss Pritt took Katharine's elbow, led her to the bathroom, and stood her in front of the toilet. "If you're going to be sick, you needn't stand in the middle of the nursery. I will see to Oswald and be right back."

Katharine closed the door and bit her nails awhile.

There was a knock. "How are you, Katharine?" came Miss Pritt's voice.

"I d-did vomit," said Katharine.

"I'm sorry. Let me in."

Miss Pritt asked Katharine a lot of embarrassing questions about her digestion. She went away and came back with a bottle and a spoon. She poured dark brown syrup into the spoon. The smell was vile.

"No, Miss Pritt—I can't swallow that."

"Yes."

"No."

"*Yes*. It's for your own good."

Katharine submitted, finally, as Miss Pritt poured the liquid into her mouth. Katharine swallowed. The vile liquid sent a shudder through her.

Miss Pritt was filling the spoon again. "Another."

"No, Miss Pritt." Tears filled Katharine's eyes.

"Katharine, listen to me. I am in charge of you. How will I explain to your parents that you did not allow me to take care of you?"

Miss Pritt forced Katharine to swallow the second dose. "Now, was that really so awful?" said Miss Pritt. "Good girl. Come and sit on your bed." Miss Pritt remained with Katharine for some time. And then, of all things—after all the talk of being sick—she vomited on her bedroom floor. Miss Pritt led her, weeping, to the bathroom.

Katharine heard a discussion going on outside. Lottie, who had been taking care of Oswald, didn't want to clean up the mess. Neither did the day maid. Miss Pritt said it was not her job.

Katharine stood over the toilet. She really did feel sick. She wanted her mother. No one cared about her. They were just fighting over the mess she had made. Oh, how she missed dear Mrs. Hodkins!

After a while, Katharine went back to her bedroom. Someone had cleaned up. She could hear Miss Pritt calling Freddie. What a distraction Katharine had been! Miss Pritt stopped in her doorway. "Have you seen your brother?"

"I think he's in the garden."

"He is not. I've looked there." She eyed Katharine. "You're hiding something from me. Where is he?"

Katharine didn't know what to say, so she said, "Maybe at the candy store."

"What, without my permission? Now I have to hunt for my charge in the streets? He'll answer for this." She started to go, then turned back. "How are you feeling?"

"I'm better. All better," Katharine assured her.

"You've gotten some poisons out of your system. I believe in that medicine." She left.

Katharine gripped the bed, wondering where Freddie was. He'd been gone too long. She wasn't going to take any more medicine.

She waited and waited. At last Freddie appeared. Katharine jumped from her bed. "How could you leave me so long?" she cried. "It was awful. She gave me horrid medicine. And I *did* get sick." She kicked him. Freddie was pushing her away when Miss Pritt entered.

"Frederick—fighting a girl again? Stop it." Miss Pritt pulled him to her by his collar. "You needn't be angry at Katharine just because she told me you went to the candy store." There was a sharp sound. Miss Pritt had slapped Freddie. A wide red mark formed on his cheek. "That will teach you not to go out without permission."

Katharine's anger vanished. She was sorry. But when Miss Pritt went to tend to Oswald, Freddie only smiled.

"Katharine, you were brilliant," he said. "I don't mind your saying I went to the candy store. It got her into the streets instead of prowling around the house. And I don't mind your kicking me. Only look at the bruise on my shin. I managed to do so much! My mouse's name is Jack."

"Why Jack?"

"Because he's 'Jack, be nimble, Jack, be quick.' I can't wait for you to see him." But of course they had to wait.

There was no park that day. Freddie was being punished, and Katharine was recovering. In the evening they were working on the sky section of the puzzle when Lottie came to clear away the supper plates.

"There's a frightful commotion downstairs," she said. "There's been another theft—two crates of wine. Mr. Sloat has just discovered it. Some wine bottles were lying on the floor, out of their crates—that's how he found out someone had been there."

"I'll have a look," said Miss Pritt, taking Oswald with her. "Work on the puzzle, children. I'll be gone only a little while."

"Now's our chance," said Freddie when Miss Pritt was gone. "All that's missing are two wine crates. I was a bit messy about emptying them. I put most of the bottles into other half-full crates; but then I was afraid I was running out of time, and I quit. Never mind. Come up, then!"

Up they went to the secret room, where Freddie lit the lamp. "Well, what do you think?" he asked, looking proud.

Jack was in a wooden wine crate. Newspaper lined the bottom. Leaves, grass, and some old rags were in a corner for him to make into a nest. Freddie had borrowed another marble ashtray and filled it with water.

"I wish we didn't have to take it," he said. "But Jack needs it."

"He's just darling," said Katharine, clapping her hands. "Hurrah! Oh, look at all the food you've taken." The shelves were filled with part of a ham, plums, cake, and jars of fruit juice.

"I had so much time," said Freddie. "You were a great distraction. And Eloise wasn't in the kitchen. Ever since Mother and Father left, she's always with the other servants in their room behind the pantry."

Katharine bunched up some pillows and let her Alice take flying leaps over them. "Oh, Freddie!" she said in horror. "You took Father's clock!"

"Well, we need one, don't we? We live according to Miss Pritt's schedule. We *have* to know what time it is. Father can buy another clock with Uncle Harry's money." Freddie pointed at a second wine crate. "I took it for the next pet. We're going to have a menagerie up here."

"Two pets are enough," said Katharine, thinking that Freddie had gotten carried away borrowing things.

Freddie picked up Jack. He knew how to hold the small, trembling mouse so it couldn't bite him. "Soon you'll be used to me," he cooed. "I'll bring you the best meats and cheese in the house. Night-night."

When they returned to the nursery, it was empty. They continued down the back stairs and listened to the voices coming from the pantry. Mr. Sloat, Gifford, and Miss Pritt were talking. It seemed the two crates had held Uncle Harry's best wine.

"Whoever did this," Mr. Sloat was saying, "knew what he was up to. That wine cost a fortune."

"Oh, Freddie," groaned Katharine. "Why did you have to take the crates with the best wine in them?"

"I looked at the dates on the bottles," whispered Freddie. "I was careful. Everything else was 1901, 1900, 1899. I thought that 1880 would be the old stuff—probably rotten. Oh, dear!"

"Can't we put the crates back and find the bottles?"

"No, we can't risk it. It would look too suspicious. Hush. What are they saying?"

Miss Pritt's haughty voice had interrupted Mr. Sloat. "Now the butler at the Pospinwall house—what a huge strong man he is. No burglar could get past him or would even dare to enter the house."

"Mr. and Mrs. Outwater will be back tomorrow

morning," said Gifford. "I've received a telegram. I'll be going to the station at nine."

"At last," whispered Katharine.

Her joy was lessened when Miss Pritt said, "Mr. Outwater has already gone to the police about the silver, the Oriental rug, and other missing articles. I expect he'll be down to the police station first thing to report this theft."

·12·

OTHER and Father were back, and once again the house was brightly lit and bustling with activity. They had brought presents: books for Katharine and Freddie, another stuffed bear for Oswald, and motoring goggles for everyone.

"Now, Miss Pritt, you must take a few days off. Start today," said Mother. "The children have exhausted you."

"We had a trying day yesterday," said Miss Pritt. She described Katharine's illness and cure. Mother and Father hugged Katharine, who was quiet. She felt on safer ground when the subject—including Freddie's disappearance—was dropped.

Miss Pritt spoke of the wine theft. She added, "Eloise says food is missing, too, but in my opinion she eats it herself." Then she announced, "Sir, Lottie has discovered that the clock in your library is gone."

"What? My clock—the one that was my father's? I can't believe it." Father left the nursery to see for himself, and came back looking as if he had lost his dearest friend. "The clock is gone. It was my father's favorite possession; it reminds me of him. I'm going to the police—I've already made one complaint, and they have done nothing about it." He rushed away.

Katharine had a vision of the police searching the house and arresting her and Freddie. She must have looked worried, because Mother said, "Don't be alarmed, my poor darling. Father will get to the bottom of this. Where is your smile, Katharine? Don't you have faith in him?"

Katharine managed a weak smile.

"Miss Pritt," continued Mother, "you had your hands full yesterday. All the more reason for you to take some time off. Why don't you pay your aunt a surprise visit?"

Mother seemed in a great hurry to get rid of Miss Pritt, and appeared as excited as Katharine and Freddie were when Gifford drove Miss Pritt to the railroad station. "What should we do with our precious time together?" she asked.

Father, who had changed from his traveling clothes into a dark suit for his visit to the police, was back. "You should not have sent Miss Pritt away," he said. "You've forgotten the interview Mrs. Pospinwall arranged for you with that newspaper—the *Daily Mail*— to publicize that dance you're on the committee of, the Orphans' Ball. You're to talk to a Mr. Lawnings at the *Daily Mail* office at half past two."

Mother's face fell. "It's going to spoil our whole day."

"Lottie can take care of the children," said Father.

"Be there on time—it's important. I'm off to the police." He left.

Mother made a face. "Oh, children, I'm sorry. How times have changed. My mother never wanted her name in the papers." Suddenly her face brightened. "I know! I'll take you all with me. It will be educational. You've never seen a newspaper office. We'll go for a picnic first."

"Miss Pritt never took us on one real outing," said Katharine.

"Oh, dear! I suppose it's harder for a nurse to arrange these things. It's all the more reason for us to go."

They all dressed up for the interview. Mother covered herself with her duster and motoring hat and put a straw hat with purple grapes in her lap. Then Gifford drove them over the Brooklyn Bridge, past rows of brownstones and on to a country road with fields and forests. They stopped at a sheltered spot.

"It's lovely to be in the country again," exclaimed Mother, "away from the crowds." She left her fancy hat on the seat of the Benz and chose a place to picnic in the shade of some fruit trees. Gifford remained behind, tightening the nuts and bolts of the Benz.

The time flew by. Suddenly Gifford approached them. "Madam, it's time to go," he said. "But I'm afraid your hat—it's met with a disaster."

"What could have happened?" asked Mother. "It was safe on the front seat."

They followed Gifford to the Benz. A short distance away, lying in the grass, were the remains of Mother's hat. Farther on, a goat was walking down the hill with wooden grapes hanging from its mouth.

"Oh, no! A goat has eaten my hat," cried Mother. She picked it up. It was ripped in front and had lost all its trim. "Gifford, where were you?"

"I was sitting in the shade," he said, twisting his cap in his hands. His eyes looked puffy.

Mother looked at him keenly. "It looks more as if you have been sleeping. I must go home for another hat."

"I'm afraid there's no time for that," said Gifford. "It's two o'clock. Your appointment is at two-thirty downtown. We can't make it. There's too much traffic."

"Oh, gracious, I can't go without a hat," cried Mother.

Freddie took the mangled hat from her. "Don't worry, Mother. I'm going to fix it for you."

Mother shook her head. "No, it's impossible to fix," she said. "I'll have to miss the interview. Father will be furious." She buried her face in her hands.

"Mother, look," said Freddie. He broke small branches off a mulberry tree laden with green, unripe fruit, pale lavender berries, and even a few deep purple ones that had ripened in that sheltered spot. He attached them to the ripped brim of the hat with a piece of rusty wire he had found. The rip was covered, but now the ugly wire showed.

"It looks beautiful," said Katharine. "Some of the mulberries are just the color of your dress, Mother. Here, take my sash to cover the wire." She pulled the pink sash from her low-waisted dress. Freddie wound it around the hat and tied a bow at the back. He handed the hat to Mother.

She examined it, frowning, and then suddenly she broke into a smile. "It's prettier than before," she said. "I'll wear it. What good care my children take of me! Let's go, then."

They took a different, shorter way back, but the road had a muddy patch. Suddenly the Benz skidded into a ditch.

"Oh, dear," said Mother. She removed her goggles. Her eyes brimmed with tears.

Katharine squeezed the bulb of the horn. Its blast was heard by two farmers plowing a field. Their horses pulled the automobile out of the ditch and down the road to where it was drier, but all this took time. It was three-thirty when the Benz pulled up in front of a building with DAILY MAIL on a sign above the door.

Mother removed her duster. "We're an hour late," she said, hastily tucking her curls under her hat.

"You look beautiful," said Freddie, staring up at the hat rather than at Mother.

"Now, children, be very polite," whispered Mother as they were ushered up some stairs to an office. Katharine held Oswald's hand tightly. She planned to be as polite as she had ever been in her life.

"Mrs. Outwater," said a bald man. "I'm Jack Lawnings. We've been waiting for you." He looked surprised to see Katharine and Freddie and Oswald.

An elegant lady was sitting very straight and stiff in

a chair. Mr. Lawnings said, "I believe you know Mrs. Armitage from your committee."

Mother greeted Mrs. Armitage, but the prim lady nodded without smiling, clearly annoyed by Mother's lateness.

"May I present my children?" said Mother. Katharine did an excellent curtsy. "I thought they would enjoy seeing a newspaper office." This was met by silence. "I'm terribly sorry to be late," she added. "We were delayed by an unexpected visitor."

"A goat," said Katharine.

"That's right," said Mother, looking embarrassed. "Remember, children, Mr. Lawnings is going to interview me, not you."

"Do sit down," said Mr. Lawnings, waving at a dirty sofa. Katharine and Freddie sat down and forced Oswald to sit between them.

Mother sat next to Mrs. Armitage, and Mr. Lawnings asked them many questions about the Orphans' Ball, which was going to raise thousands of dollars for children who had no mothers and fathers. Mrs. Pospinwall was the head of the ball. Katharine now understood why this interview was so important to Father.

Mother said she had visited the orphanage. "I will visit the orphans often from now on," she said. "It is a pity the government does not spend more money on them."

Katharine studied Mrs. Armitage. Mother had told them she was a famous beauty. Mrs. Armitage had very white skin and very black hair. It was pulled back tightly under a hat with a yellow bird on top. Katharine thought Mother's hat was much more beautiful.

Mr. Lawnings said, "Mrs. Outwater, you seem to have strong ideas about the government. Do you believe women should vote?"

"*I'm* against it," said Mrs. Armitage. "It's none of our business. Let the men vote. We belong in the home, taking care of our children. I see Mrs. Outwater has a great interest in her children. I'm sure she will agree with me."

Mother flushed pink and shook her head. "I do *not* agree," she replied. The mulberries on her hat shook. A ripe mulberry plopped into her lap and left a purple mark on her dress before rolling to the floor.

Katharine looked at Freddie. He had moved to the edge of his seat as if to catch the mulberry. Mother hadn't noticed. She was too busy arguing with Mrs. Armitage.

A man came in and set up a camera on rods. Mr. Lawnings asked Mother and Mrs. Armitage if they would be so kind as to allow a few photographs. "Our readers would like a picture, and it would help publicize the Orphans' Ball. We'll put it in the paper tomorrow. The next day, we'll run an article on Mrs. Pospinwall."

Mother nodded. Mrs. Armitage sat straighter and stiffer than ever.

"Good. Then let's continue our discussion," said Mr. Lawnings. "Are women able to understand the problems of our government?"

"Certainly not," said Mrs. Armitage.

"Certainly *yes,*" said Mother, with fire in her eyes. "I am sending my daughter to the new Stimson School, where she will get an education the equal of any boy's!" Mother gave Mrs. Armitage a triumphant look and pushed back the brim of her hat, forgetting about the mulberries. Katharine watched, horrified, as the brim crushed some of the mulberries. Mother didn't notice. She was staring down Mrs. Armitage. A stream of purple liquid trickled through the hole in the brim and down her cheek.

Click! went the camera.

"Oh!" gasped Katharine and Freddie.

Mother realized something was wrong. She wiped her cheek with her white glove and started when she saw the purple stain on it. "Oh, Mr. Lawnings," she said, standing up. "I must be on my way. My children, you know. It's time for their t-tea. It's been a pleasure chatting with y-you, Mrs. Armitage. Good day, Mr. Lawnings. Come along, children."

Katharine yanked Oswald up and followed Mother to the door. A sprig of mulberries fell to the floor. Oswald picked it up and ate a berry, smacking his lips. He handed the rest to Mother at the door.

"Here, Mama, eat," he said.

"Thank you," said Mother, looking terribly embarrassed. They walked quickly down the stairs and out to the motorcar. When the Benz had jerked forward, Mother said, "Oh, darlings, I've made a mess of it. What is Father going to say? A photo of me with mulberry juice running down my face! What will they write? They'll make such fun of me. It's just the kind of thing they like in their horrid, gossipy newspaper."

Mother unpinned the hat and let it fly out of the car.

"But, Mother, the hat really did look pretty," said Katharine.

Mother groaned. "I'm afraid I was very foolish, Katharine," she said. "The damage has been done. Oh, dear! Mrs. Pospinwall won't like it—she has no sense of humor. Please, please don't tell Father. I can't face explaining it now. Can you keep a secret?"

"Yes," said Katharine so eagerly that Freddie jabbed her in the ribs.

"I don't know what got into me, arguing with Mrs. Armitage," Mother continued. "My dear papa always said a woman should depend upon herself. So why shouldn't she vote? But I got carried away."

They drove the rest of the way home in silence. Freddie looked hurt, as if he were being blamed because he had repaired the hat. Katharine snuggled next to Mother, trying to comfort her. Mother didn't snuggle back, as she usually did. "I'll be the laughingstock of New York society," she said as they pulled up to the house.

Katharine didn't know what New York society was, but she thought that Mother loved it more than she loved her own children.

·13·

"WE'RE GOING to celebrate," said Mother when Katharine and Freddie and Oswald bounded into the drawing room for their evening visit. Two days had gone by since the interview.

"The *Daily Mail* didn't print a thing yesterday," said Mother. "They must have decided I looked too ridiculous. Today they're writing about Mrs. Pospinwall. So I'm not going to be made a fool of, after all."

"That's wonderful," said Freddie.

Katharine hugged Mother. "I'm so glad you're not disgraced."

"Careful of my hair," said Mother. "I want to look nice for the ball tonight." Mother's hair looked odd to Katharine. It was piled high, with a necklace of pearls wound through it.

"Look what I have for you," said Mother. She pulled a napkin off a tray, revealing chocolate éclairs.

Just then Father walked in and sat down in an armchair. He was sulking.

"What's the matter, dear?" asked Mother.

"See for yourself." Father handed her the *Daily Mail*. "You're on the front page."

Mother's smile faded. She took the newspaper but didn't look at it. "That's impossible. Mrs. Pospinwall is being written about today."

"Yes. She's in the middle section."

Katharine and Freddie squeezed on either side of Mother. The front page had a large photograph of Mother and Mrs. Armitage. A thick black line zigzagged down Mother's face.

Father shook his head. "Look at you, in the shadows with some hideous line going down your cheek like a scar."

"Mubbery!" shouted Oswald before Katharine could pinch him. But she saw that it was one of those times Father was too busy with his own thoughts to listen to them.

"Why do you look so faint?" asked Father. "Let me read the article aloud. Give it to me." He took the newspaper.

"Will you please be patient?" snapped Mother. "First I must give the children their t-treat." Mother's hand shook as she put éclairs on flowered plates.

"Me, me," said Oswald.

"Wait your turn," said Mother crossly.

Katharine gripped her plate with both hands. She couldn't eat. Her poor mother was going to be the laughingstock of New York.

Father cleared his throat and read, " 'Mrs. John Armitage and Mrs. Frederick Outwater met in the

Daily Mail offices to discuss the Orphans' Ball, which will be held tonight at the Waldorf-Astoria. Mrs. Armitage was dressed in yellow silk, with a matching hat topped by a yellow bird.' Humph," grunted Father. "All those silly details for the women readers." He continued, "'Mrs. Outwater had a highly original hat of fresh mulberries.' Humph!" said Father. "What silly writing, calling them 'fresh mulberries.' One would think you could eat them."

This time Katharine pinched Oswald so hard he screamed.

"Quiet, Oswald," said Father. He read the rest of the article, then looked gloomier than before.

"That's all?" asked Mother, beginning to calm down. She had been very pale, but now the color came back to her cheeks.

Father nodded, his chin in his hands. "Rather disappointing. They report all your strong views on woman's rights, just because it's a touchy issue. How will it look to the Pospinwalls? I'm sure they think anyone who wants to give women the vote is crazy." Father sighed. He hit the newspaper with his finger. "And look at this photograph! They put you in the shadows and that pushy Mrs. Armitage in front, and they draw a freakish scar down your cheek."

"It doesn't matter in the least," insisted Mother, looking very cheerful. "You're going to become a member of Pospinwall, Butler, and Gates because you're the best man. And that's that!" She hugged Katharine and Freddie, forgetting about her hair. "Children, we can celebrate, after all."

"Celebrate what?" asked Father, but no one answered. They were all busily eating éclairs.

"Children, I know what will make you happy. I'm going to get you . . ." Mother paused. She loved to drag out surprises.

"A dog," cried Freddie and Katharine.

"No, no, no," said Mother. "We're not settled yet. I'm going to buy you goldfish for the stone pool in the garden. You may help McSweeney feed them."

Katharine exchanged a knowing look with Freddie. They had discovered a crystal punch bowl in the large cabinet in the dining room. It was never used. Freddie had said it would make an excellent aquarium. Katharine knew that at least two of the goldfish would find themselves swimming in the punch bowl in the secret room. Baby Alice, who sometimes looked so lonely, would like watching them.

With a smile Katharine held out her plate for a third éclair.

·14·

FEW DAYS LATER, Gifford dropped off Miss Pritt and Oswald at one of the great stone mansions along Fifth Avenue. They were attending a birthday party, while Katharine and Freddie were going on an outing with Lottie. Miss Pritt frowned down at Lottie. "I don't know why Madam makes everything so complicated. Just because Oswald and I are occupied, I don't see why the other two have to have an outing. Don't let them out of your sight."

"I'll watch them like a *hawk*. What do you think?" shouted Lottie. She moved to the front seat of the Benz, and Gifford drove uptown toward the fields at the outskirts of New York.

Freddie whispered to Katharine, "This is our chance to find a very special pet for the other wine crate. It's been empty too long, after all the trouble I went to to get it."

"And the trouble I went to," Katharine reminded him.

They were both bursting with confidence and had

started their night visits once more. Miss Pritt had not awakened again. They had made a great discovery about her. Oswald had come to Katharine in the middle of the night. He had a cold, and his nose was running.

"Katwin, go batwoom."

"Ask Miss Pritt."

"Sleep."

Freddie had heard their voices and gotten up. They had taken Oswald to the bathroom, and had purposely spoken in normal voices outside Miss Pritt's open door. They had made Oswald try to wake her. He even had tapped her shoulder. But this had not interrupted Miss Pritt's regular breathing.

She was a heavy sleeper. That was why they were getting away with so much. Two goldfish were now swimming in the crystal punch bowl up in the secret room. And now, as Gifford drove past a sign for 142nd Street, Katharine and Freddie were looking forward to another pet. They felt they could handle anything.

Gifford parked the Benz in a deserted spot by some fields and patches of vegetables. A few wooden houses were in the distance. "Run along, children," he said. "Have your picnic. Lottie is tired. She's going to stay here."

Lottie sat in the front seat, beet red. Katharine thought she looked sick. She and Freddie ran off as fast as their legs could carry them. Lottie did not watch them like a hawk. In fact, she didn't watch them at all.

The fields were full of wild creatures. A pretty brown rabbit with a white tail stopped a short distance from them and stared into space. Freddie squeezed Katharine's arm. There was no need to talk. They both knew this was the special pet the wine crate had been waiting for.

Freddie lay flat in the grass and moved toward the rabbit, dragging the picnic blanket with him. Katharine approached from the other side, armed with her petticoat. The rabbit didn't move until Freddie lunged. Then it hopped away at lightning speed.

It didn't matter. There were many others, even baby rabbits. Again and again they stalked them in the high grass. The Benz was a small dot in the distance. At last they cornered a baby rabbit by a stone wall. Freddie advanced from one side, and suddenly something very lucky happened. The rabbit ran straight into Katharine. She pounced on it with her petticoat. Then Freddie fell on top of her with the blanket, knocking the breath out of her. He covered the petticoat with the blanket and rolled off, his arms around a moving lump. "Get the picnic basket," he said.

Katharine dumped out the horrid "healthy" tongue sandwiches, and Freddie unrolled the rabbit into the basket. Katharine slammed the lid shut and fastened it.

They had it—the perfect pet.

They carried the picnic basket between them to the Benz and asked to go home. It was all so easy. They arrived at Uncle Harry's house at two, and had two hours to settle in the baby rabbit before Miss Pritt was due. The bottom of the wine crate was lined with Father's *Tribune*. The top was covered with chicken wire that could be opened or closed.

Unfortunately, Father's last marble ashtray had to

be taken from the library so that the rabbit could have water. They gave it a carrot, but it was too frightened to eat. Katharine and Freddie sat with the trembling little animal in their laps, fighting about whose turn it was to hold it. Its fur was so soft.

"Soon you'll be so used to us, you'll jump right into our laps," said Freddie.

"Oh, do you really think so?" asked Katharine. Alice was a disappointment that way. She always hopped away from Katharine. Jack still tried to bite. And as for their two goldfish, Sir and Madam, it was hard to get friendly with fish.

It was almost time to go downstairs. Katharine and Freddie gave themselves a decent lunch of sweets and fed their pets. They gave the rabbit a name—Princess—and lifted her out of her crate for a hop around her new home. The baby rabbit hopped straight into the fishbowl, making water splash out. The fish almost splashed out, too. Before Freddie could catch her, Princess had jumped on the shelves.

Freddie grabbed at her, but she jumped to the floor with a strong push of her hind legs. The shelves shook. Katharine watched, too far away to stop it, as a jar of orange juice fell to the floor and shattered into tiny, glittering pieces. The juice spread over the floor and wet a corner of the Oriental rug.

"Stop her!" cried Katharine.

Freddie finally caught Princess and held her under her short front legs. Her two large hind feet stuck out. "You're a naughty rabbit," he said, although he and

Katharine were laughing. Princess looked so sweet and funny.

Katharine was surprised at how much damage Princess had done in a few seconds. Was she too big a pet to have hidden away in the secret room? She was as cuddly and soft as a puppy, and they already loved her best of all the pets. But on the way downstairs, Katharine stopped and sighed.

"What's the matter?" asked Freddie.

"I've got a bad feeling about Princess," she said. "She's going to grow bigger and stronger. I'm afraid she's going to get us in trouble."

"How?" asked Freddie, as confident as ever. "Princess doesn't bark or squeak or anything. She's silent. Don't worry!"

Katharine did worry. It had been easy—too easy—to get Princess. She felt as if they had walked into a trap.

·15·

MOTHER was having a dinner party. The house had been in an upheaval for days. Day maids were dusting the furniture with feather dusters and polishing the doorknobs and shaking the rugs in the garden. Eloise was in a frenzy and had no time to give her adorable boy and Katharine cookies. She shooed them out of her hot kitchen, so they were unable to get even a piece of bread for their pets.

The evening of the party, the house blossomed with flowers and potted palms in every corner. Two new manservants appeared to help serve dinner. Mother told them, "I want every detail to be absolutely perfect." She was very excited and nervous.

A hush settled over the house as the time came for the guests to arrive. Miss Pritt sent Katharine and Freddie down in their best clothes. They found Mother and Father in the drawing room with a tall, haughty-looking woman and a short, rosy-cheeked man. Katharine did a quick curtsy.

"At last Mr. and Mrs. Pospinwall have a chance—" began Father.

"Pospinwall?" burst out of Katharine. "I've heard so much about you!"

Mrs. Pospinwall turned a lorgnette on Katharine, peering at her through the long-handled eyeglasses.

"Your children are very well behaved," continued Katharine, hoping to please her. "And I hear that your butler is very huge and strong and that no burglar would dare enter your house."

Mrs. Pospinwall scowled. Mother and Father looked embarrassed. But Mr. Pospinwall threw back his head and laughed.

"You are fortunate to have Miss Pritt." Mrs. Pospinwall sniffed. "She is the best nurse in New York."

Mother looked relieved when Oswald came in with Miss Pritt. Miss Pritt greeted Mrs. Pospinwall stiffly. Katharine was amazed; she had thought they loved each other so much.

Mother drew Katharine into the hall. "People don't like being talked about behind their backs," she whispered.

"I'll tell Miss Pritt that," said Katharine.

"You had better try to get on with her instead," said Mother, looking annoyed. "And that was not a proper curtsy you did. You embarrassed me."

The other guests were arriving. Soon Katharine was bobbing up and down, trying to remember to curtsy slowly, and saying "How do you do?" and telling everyone her name and how old she was, when asked. Then Miss Pritt sent her and Freddie upstairs with sharp little pushes in their backs. The nursery seemed quiet and gloomy after the excitement downstairs. Katharine put on her nightgown.

Suddenly Miss Pritt exclaimed, "Oswald has a fever. What a time to get sick!"

Katharine and Freddie went into his room to see him. Oswald's cheeks were very red. He started crying, "Mamaaa."

"Your mother is busy," said Miss Pritt. "Frederick, go down the back stairs and tell Lottie to bring up a large bowl and fresh towels. We haven't any. I'm going to sponge Oswald down."

"Go down in my nightshirt?" asked Freddie.

"Go."

Katharine kept Freddie company. They found Lottie in the pantry and gave her the message. Katharine opened the pantry door and peeked into the dining room. "Oh, Freddie, come and see," she called. "It's so pretty, like a picture in a fairy-tale book."

The dining room was shining with silver knives and forks and golden plates and sparkling crystal glasses. On the sideboard, at the other end of the room, was a silver bowl overflowing with fruit. Katharine thought of Princess, who had grown amazingly in the week they had had her. She had an enormous appetite and loved bananas. Perhaps she would like plums and grapes and oranges, too. Katharine tiptoed over to the sideboard, picked up the hem of her nightgown so that it made a large pocket, and filled it with fruit.

"Katharine, come back," whispered Freddie. "You'll get caught."

"No, I won't," said Katharine. "Come and help. We can feed Princess for a week. There's so much fruit, the guests can't possibly eat it all."

Freddie tiptoed in, picked up the hem of his night-shirt, and filled it with fruit. Suddenly they heard the hum of people talking. As the paneled doors opened, they ducked to the floor. The sound of talking had become a roar: the guests were entering the dining room.

For one horrified second Freddie and Katharine stared at each other. Quickly Freddie lifted the lace tablecloth and crawled under the dining table, and Katharine scrambled after him, her fruit spilling in all directions.

It had happened so fast. Katharine sat under the table, blinking her eyes in the dim light, speechless. Chairs were being pulled out, and silk skirts billowed under the table. Men's black pants and shoes appeared between the skirts.

"Look what you've done," said Freddie in a low voice. "Why did you have to get fruit for Princess?"

"I'm sorry," said Katharine. "Is dinner going to be long?"

"Yes, very long! You saw all those knives and forks."

Katharine sighed. She noticed a lavender skirt at the head of the table. "That's Mother," she told Freddie. "I remember her dress."

Freddie ignored her. He had stretched out between the two sets of table legs, carved at the base in the shape of animal paws. He took up the entire center space under the table. He was eating a banana. Now that Katharine's eyes were used to the darkness, she saw that her grapes were next to a man's foot. As she watched, he moved his foot and crushed a bunch of them.

"I'm going to rescue the rest," she whispered.

"Don't!" Freddie squeezed her arm. "I'll *die* if they discover me under here in my nightshirt."

"I want those grapes. I'm hungry. Stop digging your nails into me." She shook off his hand and saved the grapes that were not under the man's foot. Now the man started moving his foot back and forth over the remaining slimy grapes as if they were bothering him. His hand picked up the lace tablecloth. Katharine backed away just in time. The man kicked the grapes. They sailed through the air and landed on Freddie's chest. The lace cloth dropped down again.

Katharine laughed aloud, but Freddie was furious. He picked up the wet, slimy grapes and dropped them in Katharine's lap. "Here. You wanted to eat them."

"That's mean," whispered Katharine. She put the grapes between the toes of a table leg. Freddie was taking up all the room in the center. She slapped his leg. "Move over."

"Stop hitting me," Freddie said as he pushed her. Katharine almost fell between a man's knees. She pushed Freddie back, throwing all her weight into it. He fell against the mahogany leg. The table shook, and glass clinked overhead. They both froze, looking up at the wooden tabletop. It had become silent overhead.

"I'm terribly sorry, Mrs. Renntree," said Mother.

"Excuse me, madam," said Mr. Sloat. "I'll put these

napkins on the wine. Thank you. Here is another glass."

"This calls for more wine," said Father. Everyone laughed and began talking again.

"See? You spilled wine," said Freddie.

Katharine didn't want to fight. She gathered her fruit and moved over to Mother. There was a sound: *bzzzz*.

"You called, madam?" That was Mr. Sloat.

"No," said Mother.

Katharine ate a plum and spit out the pit.

"This is delicious trout," said a fat man sitting next to Mother. Katharine knew he was fat because she had an excellent view of his stomach. She crawled back to Freddie and told him they were on the fish course.

Freddie groaned. "They've still got to eat the meat course and the salad course and dessert. I wish they'd stop talking so much and just eat." He glared at Katharine.

Katharine sat with her head in her hands. She could never sit still for long. And now she couldn't even talk to Freddie, he was so angry. It wasn't her fault that the little rabbit ate so much. Princess was too big for the secret room. Every time they let her out of her crate, she upset things. She loved to burrow under the silk pillows, as if to make a nest, and she chewed the tassels, which worried Katharine. After all, the pillows were only borrowed. Katharine sighed and reminded herself that it was a great adventure having the little rabbit upstairs.

"Katharine, want to play?" asked Freddie. He crouched between the table legs.

"Yes!"

Freddie placed a peach between one set of table legs and held an orange in his hand. "Get your orange," he said. "We'll roll them to the peach, and whoever gets closest gets a point."

This kept them busy until Freddie's orange rolled under a lady's gray skirt. He had won fifty-eight points to Katharine's forty-two. He slowly lifted the gray skirt, then reached in and moved his hand about.

"Freddie, don't," whispered Katharine.

His hand came out with the orange, and he smiled at it. Just then the lady in gray kicked the man on her left and the man on her right. Both men rubbed their sore legs.

Katharine and Freddie collapsed on the floor, stifling their laughter with their hands. Katharine decided it was time to crawl back to Mother. The fat man could be counted upon to be talking about food. "The Europeans make the best salads," he was saying. "We Americans don't know what a good salad is."

"Oh, no?" asked Mother, sounding polite but uninterested.

Katharine crawled back to Freddie to give him the news.

"Only the salad?" moaned Freddie. They sat quietly, eating their fruit. There was nothing else to do. Katharine, restless, returned to Mother.

Again there was that sound: *bzzzz*.

"Madam, I was just going for the cake," said Mr. Sloat.

"Good gracious, I didn't call you," said Mother, sounding annoyed.

"Madam, you did call."

"Mr. Sloat, I know very well whether I called you or not," said Mother.

Katharine motioned to Freddie to come closer. "They're about to start dessert," she whispered. "Hurrah!"

Bzzzz.

"Madam, this time you rang," said Mr. Sloat.

"I did, did I?" snapped Mother. "I know very well when I am ringing." She brought her toe to a little bump in the carpet right next to Katharine's knee. Katharine jumped away. She had been leaning on the buzzer that had just been installed. The wires went under the carpet to the kitchen. She showed it to Freddie. "Don't touch that. It's the buzzer."

"It is not," said Freddie. "Father put the buzzer near him. That's just a bump in the carpet." He pressed it.

Bzzzzzzzz.

"Yes, madam?" It was Mr. Sloat again.

"Well, Mr. Sloat, you're back again," said Mother, sounding furious. "I assure you I did not buzz. But tell me, what in the world is Miss Pritt doing standing in the doorway? Please ask her to leave, unless there is something serious."

"You've gotten us into so much trouble!" exclaimed Freddie.

Katharine was so nervous that she ate the last piece of Princess's fruit, a hard, unripe pear. The fat man took off his shoes and wiggled his toes right under her nose. His big toe was sticking out of a hole in his sock. Katharine moved away, but suddenly the man near her stretched out his legs, practically sticking his feet in her lap. Another man was kicking his foot back and forth. There was hardly a safe spot under the table.

"They're restless," said Freddie, "and I don't blame them. Why don't they get up?"

Finally they did. The chairs moved. Skirts rustled. Everyone stood up. In another moment the dining room was silent. Katharine and Freddie peeked out. The room was deserted. They crawled out and stood up. Then Katharine gasped. She was looking a waiter in the eye. He seemed as surprised as she was.

"Come on," said Freddie.

Katharine ran past the waiter and through the pantry door, then up to the safety of the nursery.

Father, Mother, and Miss Pritt were standing in the middle of the room.

"Thank God, you're all right," said Father. "Where have you been? Miss Pritt has been looking for you for two hours."

"Speak up," said Mother. "We have guests to attend to downstairs."

"Madam, they're thinking up a lie. I can see it in their faces," said Miss Pritt.

"I'm not!" answered Freddie. "We were under the dining-room table."

There was a stunned silence. Katharine was as sur-

prised as anybody. It had never occurred to her to tell
the truth, but she quickly realized it was the best thing
to do. After all, the waiter had seen them.

"Katharine wanted to look at the table," said Freddie. "When the guests came in, we didn't want to be
seen in our nightclothes, so we crawled under."

"So it was you pressing the buzzer," cried Mother.
"Mr. Sloat nearly drove me to distraction."

"That was Katharine. She wanted to sit near you,"
said Freddie. Katharine could see he was still angry
with her.

"You shook the table," said Mother. "You spilled
the wine on poor Mrs. Renntree."

"He did it," said Katharine.

"Because she pushed me!"

"It sounds as if you were fighting under there," said
Father. He covered his mouth. "Did you see anything
interesting?"

"Yes," said Katharine. "The fat man near Mother
took off his shoes, and he had a huge hole in his sock."

Father laughed. "Mr. Bowles! My dear Katharine,
he's rich enough to buy all the socks in this country."

Katharine wished Mother would laugh, but she
didn't. "We must go down to our guests," she said.
"Miss Pritt, I'm grateful to you for taking such good
care of Oswald. Thank heavens, his fever is down."
She shook a finger at Katharine and Freddie. "I'll talk
to you in the morning. You spoiled my dinner party."
She and Father rushed away.

Miss Pritt's chest was going up and down. "You'll
pay dearly for this," she said. "I have never been so

humiliated in my life. Having to hunt for my charges all over the house!"

Katharine didn't hear the rest. Her stomach had tied itself in a painful knot. Miss Pritt, of course, had a remedy—a spoonful of Dr. Siepert's Genuine Angostura Bitters to settle stomach cramps. At least it was not the vile brown syrup Miss Pritt had given her before. Katharine felt so guilty about ruining Mother's party that she submitted and swallowed the spoonful. It tasted awful.

That night she tossed and turned in bed, and ran often to the bathroom. She shouldn't have eaten all that fruit. She couldn't go to Mother's room; Mother was angry. She had ruined Mother's dinner party. How could she have done this to Mother, whom she loved so much? It was all because of Princess and trying to keep up with her enormous appetite.

Katharine admitted something to herself. Princess was a disappointment. The little rabbit didn't like to be cuddled. All she cared about was food. She didn't take the place of a dog at all. Besides, it was very unpleasant having to pick up her wet, soggy newspapers with all those hard round droppings and sneak them out to the garbage cans. The contrary thoughts that she had tried to stop under the dinner table now took over.

I wish we hadn't taken Princess, she thought, but she didn't dare tell Freddie this. He would call her a coward for wanting to quit when things got difficult.

The clock struck two. Freddie tiptoed into her room.

He was sick, too. "Katharine?" he whispered. "Want to go upstairs? We might feel better with the pets."

"*No!*" burst out of Katharine.

Freddie went back to bed. He probably thought she was too sick to go. But Katharine knew something had changed. She didn't want to keep Princess any longer. And she had another contrary thought: it smells up in the secret room with all the pets. It *stinks*.

·16·

KATHARINE felt a little better in the morning, but not well enough to eat much of the sticky oatmeal Miss Pritt put in front of her and Freddie and Oswald. She had managed to get a little oatmeal down when Mother came into the nursery.

"In the light of day, sitting under the table does seem like a harmless prank," she said. "I forgive you."

Katharine flung herself into Mother's arms.

"Mind you," added Mother, "I nearly had a fight with Mr. Sloat over the buzzer. And Lottie has been complaining all morning about a horrid mess of fruit skins and pits under the table."

The mention of fruit made Katharine's stomach flip-flop.

"Madam, excuse me, but you are disrupting the discipline of the nursery," said Miss Pritt through tight, pursed lips. "I plan to confine Katharine and Frederick to the nursery for the entire day as a punishment."

Mother flushed pink. She swept the hair out of her face as she always did when she was angry. "Oswald is well," she said. "They may all go to the park as usual. It's too hot to stay inside. I repeat, they are forgiven." Mother looked Miss Pritt in the eye.

"Very well, madam," said Miss Pritt, lowering her eyes.

Mother had won! Katharine was overjoyed. She would show Mother how right she had been to forgive her.

Mother took Katharine's hands from around her waist. "Darling, I've got an appointment. Life is so tiresome with all these social duties." She rushed down the hall.

"We'll never embarrass you again!" shouted Freddie. "I swear it . . . upon my honor." He must have been thinking of King Arthur, although it was a long time since Father had read to them.

"We're going to be so good. I swear it!" called Katharine.

And they were; they were very good. However, Katharine wondered if anyone noticed. The household was soon in an uproar again, preparing for another, bigger party in honor of Mother's uncle Oswald. It was very soon after the last party, but it couldn't be helped. Uncle Oswald had chosen this moment to visit from the West, and he was very dear to Mother, for he was the brother of her beloved papa. Uncle Oswald loved music, so a musicale had been planned. Mother had hired two singers from the Metropolitan Opera to perform. After the music an elaborate buffet cooked by Eloise would be served.

"I do so hope to impress Uncle Oswald with our life

here," said Mother. "I want him to be proud of me, and I want you children to make an excellent impression."

On the day of the party all the armchairs and sofas in the drawing room were moved into rows facing the piano, with rented gold chairs placed in between; and the house bloomed once more with flowers and potted palms. While they were waiting for the guests to arrive, Katharine and Freddie worked on the puzzle. The sky and fields were complete. Only the village remained to be done, a large hole in the middle.

Suddenly Mother appeared in the nursery, still in her dressing gown. "Miss Pritt," she announced, "there's a crisis downstairs. The punch bowl is missing. The punch is made, and there's nothing to put it in."

Katharine looked at Freddie. He was staring at a piece of thatched cottage in his hand. Poor Mother! Katharine thought. They were spoiling her party again.

"Miss Pritt, please go down and find a container for the punch," pleaded Mother. "Lottie can't deal with it, and you know how excitable Eloise is. You're the only one with a head on your shoulders."

"Very well, madam," said Miss Pritt, taking Oswald's hand. "There's been another burglary, in my opinion."

"Oh, let's not discuss that now," cried Mother, flinging up her hands and running down the hall.

Miss Pritt and Oswald went down to the kitchen. Katharine and Freddie listened on the back stairs. Everyone was screaming and accusing one another of having broken or stolen the punch bowl. Katharine and

Freddie didn't wait to hear any more. They raced up to the secret room with slugs and lettuce and cheese. At this party, Miss Pritt had told them, she was going to watch them closely. They would not get another chance to feed the pets.

Freddie took Princess out of the crate. "It's your turn to clean," he said, opening Katharine's diary to the page entitled CLEANING RABBIT BOX with their names and check marks underneath.

Katharine made a face. "All right, but hold her. I'm letting Alice have a hop around." She put her frog next to the punch bowl to watch Sir and Madam. "Poor Mother," she said, pointing to the punch bowl.

Freddie nodded. "We'll have to have extra-good manners tonight to make up for it."

Katharine gathered Princess's soggy, smelly newspapers, bunched them in a corner to take out later, and replaced them with Father's *Times*. She hadn't said anything to Freddie yet about freeing Princess. She kept hoping Freddie would bring it up.

Suddenly Princess wriggled out of Freddie's arms and hopped right over Alice.

"Oh, Freddie," Katharine said. "She nearly killed Alice!" The little frog disappeared behind the pink pillows. But Freddie was gripping Katharine's arm, his face pale, his eyes popping.

"Kaaaatharine! Freeeederick!" Miss Pritt was calling them. She sounded as if she were on the floor below.

Freddie banged open the door. "Come on, Katharine!"

But Katharine couldn't find Alice. She threw up all the pillows and found her under one of them. She tossed Alice in her box, threw the veil over it, and scrambled out after Freddie. They left the secret door to close itself. Miss Pritt met them at the bottom of the stairs.

"What on earth are you doing up in the attic?" she demanded. She didn't wait for an answer. "Do you intend to keep your great-uncle waiting? He has arrived." When she was satisfied with Freddie's tie and Katharine's bow, she ushered them into Father's library. A tiny, wrinkled man with a stringy white beard was talking to Mother and Father. He had the same sparkling blue eyes as Mother's papa.

"Darlings, come and meet Uncle Oswald," said Mother. Katharine curtsied as gracefully as she could.

Uncle Oswald smiled at her. He took her hand and held it in his wrinkled one and didn't let it go. "My dear, you look just like your mother when she was your age," he said. He had a very hoarse voice.

Mother said, "Katharine doesn't believe me when I tell her. And the photographs I have are from much later."

"She's as skinny as a string bean, just like you were," croaked Uncle Oswald. Katharine didn't mind too much being called a string bean by Uncle Oswald, because he smiled in such a kind way.

He said to Freddie, "You are a fine, strapping lad."

"Thank you, sir," said Freddie, bowing for the second time. He was making a great effort to be polite.

Uncle Oswald said a few words to his namesake,

Oswald, but did not seem very interested in babies. He turned back to Katharine. Still holding her hand, he said, "I have a portrait of your mother when she was your age. I'm going to send it to you." He smiled, but Katharine didn't smile back. Something brown and furry had hopped down the hall into the drawing room!

"Katharine, what is the matter with you? What do you say to Uncle Oswald?" asked Mother.

Katharine stared blankly at her.

"Say thank you, silly," said Mother.

"Thank you." Katharine pulled her hand away from Uncle Oswald's.

"Katharine! Stop backing away!" said Mother. "I want my friends to meet you." The library was filling up with people. Soon Katharine was bobbing up and down to ladies and gentlemen, and Freddie was bowing.

At last Katharine was able to cup her hand to Freddie's ear and say, "I just saw Princess run into the drawing room."

"What?" gasped Freddie. "Didn't you put her in her box?"

"Didn't you?"

"Oh . . . oh! This is terrible. We must get her!"

They pushed past guests to the door, which Miss Pritt was guarding. "Stay right where you are," she said. "I'm not letting you out of my sight. We must wait for Oswald." Oswald was in Mother's arms, being fussed over by several people.

Then Freddie's face brightened. "I have to talk to Mother and Father," he said. He and Katharine squeezed their way back through the crowd to Mother and Father.

"May we please listen to the music?" asked Freddie. "We'll be very quiet. I've discovered that I love music!"

"I love it!" said Katharine, understanding what Freddie was up to and thinking that he was very clever.

Mother turned to Miss Pritt, who had followed them. She really was sticking to them. "Miss Pritt, it would be a very good experience for them," she said.

Father was beaming. "I'm so glad they are developing some cultural interests." He slapped Freddie on the back. "You may stay for the concert."

"May we sit in the drawing room now?" asked Katharine, trying not to sound too eager. Father nodded.

Mother tried to give Oswald to Miss Pritt, but he clung to Mother. "Oh, Miss Pritt, please give him some chocolates," she said. "Just this once." Oswald was screaming and kicking his legs.

Katharine and Freddie slipped out of the library and across the hall into the drawing room. A plump lady in a pink satin gown was standing by the piano. Four men in black ties were arranging sheets of music on stands.

"We've come to hear the concert," said Freddie.

"You are early," said a man with a thick brown mustache. He frowned at them. "Wouldn't you prefer to return in a few minutes?"

They shook their heads.

"Do sit down, then," he said. The other men took out their instruments and played some notes.

Katharine and Freddie sat on a sofa. Katharine's

eyes swept the room. There were so many places where Princess could hide. Katharine bent down and peered under the fringe of the sofa. Freddie stood up and looked behind the curtains, pretending to look out the window. Katharine moved to another sofa and ducked her head under it. She sat up and met the stare of the man with the mustache.

"Are you looking for something?" he asked.

"No, I'm trying to find a comfortable seat," she said.

"I would think you would leave those for your elders," said the man.

Katharine sat still, not daring to move for a moment. Then she stuck her foot under the lace cloth covering a table. She moved her foot around but felt nothing soft and furry. Had Princess already left the room?

The guests drifted into the drawing room and seated themselves. Freddie and Katharine sat on rented chairs in the second row. Katharine smiled at Father, who was beaming at them from the back of the room.

Uncle Oswald headed straight for Katharine and sat in an armchair next to her. "I'm very fond of music, too," he said.

A hush fell over the room as the mustached man bowed. "We are fortunate to have with us this evening two stars of the opera, Miss Edith Wharf and Mr. Jeremy Seed," he said. The lady in pink and a short, stout man bowed to the applause of the audience. The mustached man introduced the two violinists and a bass player, then sat down at the piano. A slight man, whom Katharine hadn't noticed before, stood by the piano and fingered the music on it.

"We will begin with a duet from Puccini's *La Bohème*," said the pianist. He started playing, joined by the violinists and the bass player. After a while the slight man raised his eyebrows and turned a page of the music. Katharine started watching his eyebrows to see when the page would be turned. There was a lot of music on the piano. This musicale was going to be very long.

Freddie gave her a pained look. "Are you *sure* you saw Princess?" he whispered.

A lady turned and put her finger to her lips. Katharine thought they were trapped again, just as they had been under the dining-room table. But this time it wasn't her fault. She tried to remember what had happened in the secret room. She had been hunting for baby Alice when Miss Pritt called them. Either Freddie had forgotten to put Princess back in her crate, or he had not covered the crate with the chicken wire and Princess had jumped out. They had let the secret door close slowly by itself. And Princess had escaped.

Katharine was jolted out of these thoughts by the pink lady, who had burst into song. Her dress looked like a lampshade. It had tassels hanging from the hem that shook as she sang. She was singing into the face of the short, stout man, and soon he answered her with his own very loud voice. They both looked upset and clutched their hearts.

A smile curled on Freddie's lips. He nudged Katharine. She didn't dare look him in the eye for fear she would laugh.

The stout man took the pink lady's hands, and they

sang together. Katharine thought the noise would surely rouse Princess if she was in the room. She was.

Princess emerged from the curtains behind the musicians and hopped by the skirts of the pink lady. The pink lady didn't notice, but most of the audience did—except Uncle Oswald, who had fallen asleep in the armchair. There was a murmur as heads turned and eyebrows were raised.

Katharine sat on the edge of her chair. "Should we get her?"

"I don't know," whispered Freddie. "If we get her, everyone will know she's ours."

"Oh, look what she's doing," said Katharine.

Princess was nibbling on the cuff of the page turner's pants. The page turner's eyes bulged. He shook his foot again and again, yet Princess hung on. The pianist finally had to stop playing and give the page turner an angry look until he turned the page.

The pink lady took a deep breath, and a long high note rolled out of her throat. Suddenly it turned into a scream. Princess was chewing a tassel on the singer's dress. Only Uncle Oswald paid no attention, letting his head sink farther into his chest.

Katharine and Freddie leaped from their seats. They squeezed between chairs and sofas to get to the front. Katharine held the rabbit while Freddie pried open her jaws. Then they carried the wriggling bundle out of the room, stepping on toes and skirts, through a sea of surprised and alarmed faces. Ladies whispered behind fluttering fans.

Father met them in the hall and led them down the

curved marble stairs to the front door. He opened it and pointed outside. "Drop it," he said.

Katharine put Princess down on the front step. The rabbit stood still a moment before hopping into the darkness. "Good-bye, Princess," Katharine whispered. She had always known the little rabbit would get them in trouble. She stood up to find Father scowling down at her and Freddie.

"I am very disappointed in you," he said in a cold, angry voice. "You have spoiled another party. Go to your rooms. Don't let me lay eyes on you again this evening."

Katharine noticed that the music was at a standstill. Mother turned away as they passed by. She didn't want to lay eyes on them, either. How could it have happened again? They had sworn to be good, but they had been bad, maybe worse than before.

·17·

THIS TIME Mother and Father stayed angry. They had a serious talk with Katharine and Freddie in the morning. Father said there had been too many pranks, and Mother said, "Am I to expect some mischief each time we entertain? What could Uncle Oswald possibly think of you now? I had so wanted you to make a good impression. Think about your behavior while we're gone."

Then Mother and Father went to the Benz, where Gifford was waiting. They were going to Long Island to see about renting a house by the ocean for the last days of July and all of August. They climbed into the backseat without kissing Katharine and Freddie good-bye. Gifford put a box on the front seat. Inside was Princess, who had been discovered chewing McSweeney's flowers. Mother and Father planned to leave her in a field. They believed Freddie's story that he had found the rabbit in the garden last night and taken it into the house to give it something to eat.

Back in the nursery, Miss Pritt said she had been

disgraced by her charges. "In all my thirty-one years as a nurse," she said, "I have never been so mortified. It all comes from your not having been punished properly last time." She locked Freddie in his room and Katharine in Oswald's, so that they would be separated and unable to speak to each other out their windows. Lunch was brought on a tray—liver, which Katharine did not touch.

In the afternoon she was taken to the park while Freddie was left with Lottie. Katharine had to sit alone on a bench. The nurses looked over at her often, as if they were talking about her. She was in disgrace.

Dinner was brought to her, too, in Oswald's room. Cold barley soup. She threw it out the window. She felt lost without Freddie. Even when she was in bed, Miss Pritt hovered outside. Katharine shouted, "Goodnight, Freddie!" and he shouted back, "Good-night!" She smothered her sobs in her pillow.

She must have dropped off to sleep, because suddenly Freddie was tapping her shoulder and telling her it was the middle of the night.

"Freddie!" She had never been so happy to see anyone in her life.

"I heard Mother and Father come back a long time ago," he whispered. "Let's go upstairs. I'm starving, aren't you?"

"Yes!"

Soon they were stuffing themselves with sugar cookies and chocolate cake in the cozy yellow light of the secret room. Everything they ate was especially tasty after the liver and barley soup.

Katharine freed Alice. As the little frog hopped around under her nightgown, the material popped out in funny places. While they laughed about this, Sir and Madam swam through the bridge Freddie had made them. "Hurrah," cheered Freddie. Everything seemed right about the secret room tonight. The little mouse, Jack, did a spinning dance on his hind legs. They clapped for him.

"Remember when Princess chewed on the page turner's pants," said Freddie, "and the pianist turned purple waiting for his page to be turned?"

They both collapsed on silk pillows in hysterics.

Katharine sat up. "Freddie, who will feed the pets when we go to Long Island?"

"I hadn't thought of that," said Freddie. "We'll have to free them."

Then Katharine said it. "I'm happy Princess is free and is going to live in a field of vegetables."

"Yes. And wait and see. By tomorrow Mother and Father won't be angry anymore."

Freddie was right. The next morning Mother was all smiles when she came into the nursery. They rushed to her, even Freddie, as if they had been separated for a year. Oswald jumped into her arms.

"We've rented a beautiful house right on the ocean," said Mother. "You will love it."

Miss Pritt was not there. Katharine and Freddie told Mother how she had locked them in their rooms.

"Good morning, madam," said Miss Pritt, entering the nursery with her sugary smile on her thin lips. "I hope your trip was pleasant. I have punished the children, as we agreed. I have kept the two of them apart so they could think seriously about their behavior. Maybe now we will see an improvement."

For a moment a look of distress clouded Mother's face. Then she said, "Children, you have been punished enough. Father and I have been talking. We've been trying to understand why you brought the rabbit in." Mother turned her beautiful eyes on Katharine and Freddie. Katharine wondered what Mother was going to say.

"It's very simple," said Mother. "You want a pet. You've asked and asked, and I've said no because we weren't settled."

Katharine's heart took a great leap.

"And so, darlings, I persuaded Father. He wanted to wait, but I told him we've waited too long. We're going to get you—"

"*A dog!*" yelled Katharine and Freddie.

"Yes." Mother could say no more for a while because everyone jumped on her and kissed her.

"I've heard of a litter of schipperke pups in Connecticut," she said. "They're not very large dogs—just right for the city—and they're very good watchdogs." She paused. "What with all the talk of thefts in our house, it's an excellent idea. Only we must hurry, before someone else picks the best pup and leaves us the runt of the litter."

Miss Pritt had been silent. Now she said, "I will not have a filthy animal in the nursery."

"Oh, we won't keep the puppy in the nursery," said Mother. "It will stay downstairs in the storage room.

Children, get your goggles. Excuse us, Miss Pritt. We'll be gone a few hours. You'll have a little time to yourself."

They all rushed downstairs, but Gifford couldn't be found. "Goodness, I forgot," said Mother. "Father gave Gifford the day off until five. We can't go. No dog today."

Mother put Oswald down on the sidewalk. He immediately began to cry. Even Freddie, who was swinging his goggles, looked as if he were blinking back tears.

"Oh, children, I can't stand to see you all so disappointed. And I can't go tomorrow—I have to visit the orphans." Suddenly Mother clapped her hands. "I know! I'll drive to Connecticut myself. Father has given me some driving lessons, and I do feel I am ready. I've always wanted to drive by myself, and now I shall do it."

They all started to follow her to the stables, where the Benz was kept. Mother shook her head. "I am not going to take passengers on my maiden voyage," she said. "Definitely not. Go upstairs to Miss Pritt and study hard. In a few days you are going to visit the schools to be tested. Only if you do well will you be accepted. So go on, and take Oswald."

Katharine and Freddie put Oswald inside the house, then waited on the sidewalk and watched for the Benz. At last Mother drove by so slowly that they could run alongside her.

"Oh, Freddie," said Mother. "How am I doing?"

"Change the gear, Mother. Go on!" The Benz was shaking.

"Yes, yes, here it is—" The motorcar jerked forward.

"Press the accelerator," said Freddie.

"Gracious, I'm going too f-fast," said Mother, although every carriage in the street was passing her. She gripped the wheel tightly. "Good-bye," she called as she turned off Madison.

"I just can't believe it," said Katharine. "I had given up hoping for a puppy. Oh, I can't wait to see it."

The time went very slowly. It was late afternoon when Katharine and Freddie, stationed at the nursery window, heard a screech and saw the Benz pull up very abruptly in front of the house. They raced down to the street.

Freddie asked, "What happened to the Benz?" The rear was crumpled, and the brass trim was dangling.

"A little accident," Mother said, getting out of the motorcar. "Let's not talk about it now. Look what I have." She opened a box and took a black bundle into her arms. "Isn't he darling?" she said. The puppy was pitch-black, with a pointed nose and pointed ears and the brightest black eyes. Katharine and Freddie crowded around Mother, petting him.

"Wait, wait." Mother laughed. "He shouldn't be outside yet. He's only a baby." They followed her into the house, and Mother put him down on the floor of the storage room. He cocked his head to one side, looking at Katharine and Freddie, and wagged his little stub of a tail.

"He's so intelligent," said Mother. "Look at him

studying you. He was the most spirited pup in the litter."

As if to prove it, the puppy took some lightning turns around the storage room and jumped on Freddie's legs. Freddie picked him up and received some wet kisses. Then it was Katharine's turn. She held the warm little puppy quietly, knowing that she loved him.

Mother went off to park the Benz in the stables. "What are you going to call him?" she asked when she returned.

"Arthur," said Freddie. "After King Arthur."

"That's a lovely idea," said Mother. "He's so well-born. His mother and father were champions. I do wish Father would finish that book. It's been a long time."

Katharine giggled. Arthur was burrowing his nose into her waist and chewing a button.

"Madam, that is a new dress." Miss Pritt was standing in the doorway with Oswald.

"Oh, Miss Pritt, isn't he sweet?" said Katharine. She wished Miss Pritt would like him, so that he could stay up in the nursery.

"It's not sweet to have your dress chewed," said Miss Pritt sourly.

Katharine put Arthur down. He bounded over to Oswald, who screamed and ran away. Arthur chased him playfully until Oswald climbed onto a trunk. Everyone laughed but Miss Pritt.

"Madam, that animal is not coming into the nursery."

"We understand," said Mother to Miss Pritt. "Be so good as to get Lottie. We'll move a few cases up to the attic and make room for Arthur here."

Soon Lottie was trudging upstairs with a heavy suitcase. Mother was in front with two cases, and Katharine and Freddie were in the rear with a trunk between them. They left Arthur in the storage room. Katharine tried not to listen to his yelps.

"Freddie, I don't like how everyone is going up to the attic," she whispered.

"Don't worry. What could possibly happen?" said Freddie.

Lottie grumbled all the way up the steps. Katharine, behind her, saw that Mother had moved the trunk that always stood in front of the secret door. When Lottie reached the top of the stairs, she was fuming. "There!" she cried, and flung the heavy suitcase against the secret door. It hit the lower boards hard, and as Katharine watched helplessly, the door opened.

·18·

KATHARINE rushed to Lottie and grabbed her by the waist, trying to pull her away.

"Mercy! Let me go, Miss Katharine," said Lottie. She kicked the door fully open and got down on her hands and knees to look in. "Madam, come and have a look," called Lottie. Mother walked past Katharine, smiling.

Katharine retreated to Freddie. "Do something," she whispered. But he just stood at the top of the stairs, his hand still on the handle of the trunk, his mouth hanging open.

Now Mother was on her hands and knees beside Lottie. She exclaimed, "How marvelous! Children, don't just stand there. Come and see. Lottie has discovered a secret room."

Freddie finally went over and tapped Mother's back. "M-Mother . . . shouldn't we all . . . uh . . . go down to Arthur?" he stammered.

"Why?" asked Mother. "We've discovered a secret room! Aren't you excited?" She crawled all the way in.

"It looks as if someone once lived here," she said. "Here are curtains, so there must be a window." She pulled the knob, and the window opened. The late-afternoon light entered the room.

Katharine, standing outside, hid her face in her hands.

"Goodness! It looks as if someone is living here right now!" cried Mother.

Katharine wished Freddie would do something. He just stood there, looking dazed.

Now Mother exclaimed, "Why, Lottie, there's our missing rug. I can't believe my eyes! Here's my punch bowl, with two goldfish in it. McSweeney and I thought a cat had eaten them."

"Madam, look at this! Remember the wine that was stolen?" asked Lottie. "Those are the two missing wine crates. Look, they say eighteen-eighty on them. Bless me if there isn't a frog in this tin."

"Oh, a mouse!" cried Mother. Lottie's behind wiggled out of the room, but Mother said, "No, come back, Lottie. The mouse is quite safe in this crate. Will you look at my plates and silverware, all in tidy rows? And all those chocolates and cakes!"

"Don't admit a thing," whispered Freddie, his hand damp and cold on Katharine's arm.

Mother had unhooked Katharine's diary from the wall. "This book looks familiar. . . ." She opened a page and read out loud, " 'Cleaning rabbit box. Katharine, Freddie'—" There was a silence. Mother turned around. *"Katharine, Freddie, come here!"* she exclaimed. "Well, I never. Lottie, get Miss Pritt."

Lottie backed out of the secret door, stood up, wagged her finger at Katharine and Freddie, and hurried downstairs. Katharine retreated to the stairs, but Mother said, "Just *where* do you think you're going? Come and explain what you've been doing here."

Katharine and Freddie bent down reluctantly and looked in the room. Mother was examining the pillows. "Mine," she said. "Oh, my word. There's Father's clock!" She fingered the curtains. "I suppose this is my petticoat?"

"No, mine," said Katharine meekly.

"Ah, but these are my veils—ripped off my best hats. Oh, I am shocked. My own children, ruining my hats. Did you imagine I could wear them without veils? Do you realize how expensive they are? And I accused poor Louisa, the day maid." She examined the blue porcelain vase. "I can't believe my eyes. You stole so many of our belongings!"

"We *borrowed* them," said Freddie.

"I call it stealing," said Mother. Katharine had always known that Mother wouldn't accept Freddie's explanation.

Mother flung up her hands. "And here I've smashed the Benz just to get you a pet, while you've already helped yourselves to all these pets." Mother's eyes widened. "Now I understand the rabbit at my musicale— it was your pet, too."

"We were going to free them all," said Freddie in a very small voice. "We were just talking about it last night. Isn't that true, Katharine?"

"Yes." It didn't sound true.

"That isn't the point. Oh, I'm so angry!" cried Mother. "Look at my punch bowl—turned into a fish tank. And you didn't even speak up when you saw me so distressed."

"I'll put the fish back now," offered Freddie.

"No, nothing is to be touched. I want Father to see this," said Mother in a shrill voice. "I shouldn't have talked Father into getting you a puppy. *You don't deserve a dog.*"

"The den of thieves," sang out Lottie, winking at Katharine and Freddie as she returned with Miss Pritt. Katharine and Freddie moved aside to make room for them. Miss Pritt bent down stiffly and looked into the secret room.

Katharine couldn't face what was coming next. She and Freddie tiptoed to the stairs. "We're just going down to see how Arthur is," said Freddie. No one was listening. Miss Pritt was saying, "In all my experience, I have never taken care of such dishonest children. I am appalled!"

Katharine and Freddie fled down the attic stairs and all the way to the ground floor. They stopped in front of the closed storage-room door. Freddie slapped his forehead. "How could this have happened?" he said. "Who would have thought Lottie would hit the secret door?"

"We've lost our secret room," said Katharine. She could hardly believe it. It had happened so fast, but already she felt an emptiness inside her. She and Freddie stood looking at each other, shaking their heads. "Mother's so angry," said Katharine.

Then they heard Arthur scratching the door. They went into the storage room and closed the door quickly behind them. Arthur was already jumping on them and wagging his stubby tail. They knelt beside him. "Now Mother's going to take him away," said Freddie.

"She can't!"

"Oh, she can. She said we don't deserve a dog."

Arthur pounced on Katharine, and she lay on her back while he licked her face no matter which way she turned.

"Sneaking off again?" Miss Pritt was suddenly towering above her, her face gray, her eyes gleaming. "Get up! Get up, I say." Her boot pushed angrily at Katharine's legs.

Katharine sat up, frightened. She had never seen Miss Pritt so excited. Arthur raced for the door. Miss Pritt slammed it shut. Arthur jumped on her skirt with his light paws, wagging his tail.

"Get off me, filthy animal," cried Miss Pritt. She lifted her foot, and her hard black boot hit the puppy's ribs. He yelped in pain.

"Miss Pritt, don't kick him," pleaded Katharine.

"He's only a puppy," cried Freddie.

"Hold your tongues. I'll do what I wish!" screeched Miss Pritt. She advanced on Katharine and Freddie. "Brats!" she screamed. "Evil children! You made a secret room just to make a laughingstock of me! I know that—do you hear? You should be whipped!" She raised her hand menacingly.

Freddie put up his arm to shield himself and backed away, with Katharine clinging to him. But just then

Miss Pritt stopped and turned. Something was pulling her skirt.

It was Arthur. He had gotten his teeth into the hem of her black dress and was backing away with his strong hind legs. *Rrrrr,* he growled.

"Let go, filthy beast," she shouted, turning her rage from Freddie and Katharine to Arthur. She kicked, but Arthur had learned. He dodged her boot, all the while yanking her skirt.

Katharine and Freddie rushed to Arthur, trying to protect him with their arms and trying to avoid Miss Pritt's boots. Freddie knelt beside him.

Miss Pritt kicked more furiously. The more excited she got, the more excited Arthur got. He growled and backed away and tugged at the skirt until there was the sound of a rip. Miss Pritt's skirt opened at the waist, showing her white undergarments. Still Arthur pulled, ripping the skirt more while Miss Pritt hung on to it.

Katharine hid her face and laughed. Wonderful Arthur! He surely must be the most spirited pup in the litter. Freddie's eyes were shining.

Suddenly Mother was in the room. Miss Pritt stopped kicking but pulled at her skirt. "Oh, let me help," said Mother. She bent over Arthur and managed to free the material. "I'm so sorry about your dress, Miss Pritt!" She held Arthur in her arms.

"Madam," said Miss Pritt, drawing herself up to her full height, trying to look dignified. But it was hard to look dignified while her white undergarments were showing. "Madam, I have never—never been so mistreated."

"She was kicking him. That's why he did it!" screamed Katharine.

"Katharine, control your temper," snapped Mother. "*You* are the one with explaining to do."

"Madam," said Miss Pritt, "I do not care to hear their excuses. I am giving notice. I am leaving." She hiked up her dress. "I will not stay another moment in this . . . this *crazy house*."

"Oh, Miss Pritt. Please don't do anything hasty," said Mother. "Let's discuss this." Arthur growled at Miss Pritt, but Mother held him firmly.

"Children, go sit in the drawing room," said Mother. "Take Oswald with you. He's just outside. Will you listen for once? *Go on!*"

They rushed out, bumping into Oswald. Katharine took his hand. "No doggy?" he asked.

"No doggy," said Katharine sadly, thinking that now Mother and Father surely would take Arthur away. She and Freddie could not help listening for a moment by the door.

"Madam, the fault is yours," Miss Pritt said. "All that visiting with you, at any time of the day or night. You didn't supervise them properly, and they used the time to steal and take care of their pets. Now, at Mrs. Pospinwall's I had complete *control* of the children."

"I beg your pardon," said Mother, raising her voice. "I've been wondering how you never noticed what the children were up to. An enormous amount of work went into that hideaway. It looks lived in. How could you, their nurse, not have been aware of it?"

159

Katharine's heart leaped. For once, Mother was crit- icizing Miss Pritt.

"We'd better go," whispered Freddie. "We don't want them accusing us of spying." They took Oswald up to the drawing room. Katharine sat on a sofa, and Freddie sat opposite her, his head sunk in his hands.

"If Miss Pritt leaves, we'll be blamed for that, too," he said.

"I don't care! I'll be so happy."

"I know." Freddie shook his head. "But it will just get us into more trouble. Miss Pritt will tell the Pospin- walls that we steal and our house is crazy. Then they won't take Father into the law firm. And wait till Father sees his clock."

Katharine began to cry.

"Oh, Katharine, stop crying."

"I can't help it," she sobbed. Now that the tears had begun, there was no stopping them. "We've lost our secret room—after *all* our hard work."

"Play horsey, Katwin!" said Oswald. He climbed into her lap. She pushed him back to the floor.

"How are we going to explain the clock?" asked Fred- die.

Katharine dried her eyes.

"How can we explain everything?" asked Freddie.

Katharine didn't have an answer.

After a while Mother came in and stood angrily above them, her hands on her hips. "Miss Pritt has left," she said. "She has packed her things and gone."

How Katharine had longed for this moment. But she knew that there was much to be unhappy about.

"She is leaving because of your secret hideaway. She says she doesn't want to be the nurse of such dishonest, spoiled children," said Mother. "She's right. You are thieves and liars. I, stupidly, have been spoiling you. Oh, you will be punished, I promise you that!"

After this explosion Mother sank into the sofa.

At last Freddie said, "Miss Pritt didn't say good-bye."

"She never liked us," said Katharine.

"Well, you didn't like her, either," Mother reminded them. "But she could have said good-bye . . . after all that time with us."

"That was bad manners," said Freddie.

"You never tried to get on with her," Mother accused. Now that Miss Pritt was gone, Katharine could admit that this was true.

Mother sighed. "Miss Pritt has been living with us day and night. Just to disappear . . . It feels as if we have been deserted."

There was a long silence. Freddie finally asked, "May we see if Arthur's all right?"

"No," said Mother firmly. "Forget Arthur until Father comes home. We will see what he is going to do about everything." She put her hand under Katharine's chin and tilted her head up to look in her eyes. "I never thought you would lie to me. Or you, Freddie." She sounded hurt. "You don't know how worried Father and I were by all the thefts in the house. We didn't tell you because we didn't want to frighten you. We thought that perhaps someone was entering the house, or that one of the servants was dishonest. Oh, it has been so unpleasant. And all the time we were worrying about you, you never worried about us."

Katharine dropped her eyes. She was too ashamed to look at Mother—sweet, trusting Mother. Katharine was surprised how ashamed she felt. She knew she had been lying and stealing every day, and she hadn't cared about the effect it had on anyone else.

"I'm so sorry, Mother. I really am," she whispered.

"We just thought of it as borrowing," said Freddie, his face covered by his hands. "I'm sorry, too."

"Tell Father that," snapped Mother.

There was another long, uncomfortable silence. Freddie went up to the nursery and returned, saying, "Miss Pritt took the puzzle. How could she? We were almost finished—just twenty-eight pieces left."

"Mama, play," said Oswald. He tried to climb on Mother.

"Play on the floor," she said, pushing him gently off.

Oswald had never been ignored this much, Katharine thought. He had nothing to play with. She took off the green sash from her dress, rolled it into a tight ball, and held it out to Oswald. "Here, catch," she said. Now that Miss Pritt was gone, it didn't matter if her dress was hanging loose like a sack. She didn't have to be dressed properly. *Miss Pritt was gone.* As they played, Katharine wondered what would happen to Arthur. She had waited so long for him.

The front door banged. Then they heard heavy steps on the marble stairs. Father was home.

·19·

"WHY ARE YOU all sitting around the drawing room? Where's your tea, Diana?" asked Father. His cheeks were flushed. "It has cooled off, and I've had such a pleasant walk up Fifth Avenue from the club." He looked at Mother and Freddie, slumped in their seats, and Katharine, who let the sash ball drop from her hand. Only Oswald greeted Father with a smile.

"By the way," continued Father, "where is Gifford? I didn't see the Benz out front, and we have to go out this evening."

Mother began to fidget in her seat. "Perhaps it isn't there because, because—"

"It's smashed," said Freddie.

"Nonsense. How can it be smashed? I gave Gifford almost the whole day off."

"Quite so," said Mother, fidgeting some more. "You see, the, er, puppy—I heard of a litter in Connecticut, and we just had to have first pick."

"What does that have to do with the Benz?" asked Father.

"Everything was f-fine," stammered Mother. "I drove easily to Connecticut. I even had some p-petrol put in at a drugstore. I found the farm, chose the—"

"What?" interrupted Father. "You drove the Benz?"

Mother nodded. "Everything was fine until I backed out of the driveway. A little t-tree did it. Amazing what a little tree can do. . . ." Mother's voice trailed off because Father had rushed out to the stables. They waited gloomily. He was soon back, looking very red in the face.

"The whole rear is destroyed," he said. "Even if it can be fixed, it won't be the same."

Mother hung her head.

"I was perfectly willing to give you more driving lessons," he said. "What was the hurry?"

He hadn't heard a word about the puppy.

"I have more bad news," said Mother. But she was interrupted by Gifford, who was standing in the doorway.

"Pardon me, sir."

"You've seen the Benz? Mrs. Outwater drove it," said Father.

"Yes, sir. I know," said Gifford. He was red in the face, too. "May I please speak with you alone, sir?"

Father walked into the hall. After a few moments he returned. "Gifford has given notice," he said. "He doesn't like his motorcar driven by other people."

"It's not *his* motorcar," said Katharine.

Mother was looking guilty, her face buried in her

hands. She looked up. "I'm afraid there's more bad news," she said. "Miss Pritt has just given notice and has already left."

"She's gone?" demanded Father, astonished.

Mother nodded.

"Why?" asked Father. "I thought she was doing such a fine job. What could have happened?"

"The children have something to show you upstairs in the attic," Mother said wearily. "It will throw a different light on things."

Father shifted his gaze to Katharine and Freddie. Katharine wished she could disappear.

"What happened with Miss Pritt, children? Why has she left? What have you done in the attic?" Katharine could think of nothing to say. Father turned to Mother. "How are we to explain this to the Pospinwalls? We have to call on them tonight. Jack has promised me an answer on joining the firm."

Mother seemed relieved by the change of subject. She jumped up. "I'll get Lottie to mind the children. Oh, darling, it's going to be the firm of Pospinwall, Butler, Gates, and *Outwater*!"

Father said, "Now, children, what do you want me to see in the attic? Quick! Show me." He mumbled to himself, "I cannot believe Miss Pritt has left so suddenly."

"Come, children," said Mother. She said to Father, "You are going to be shocked." She took Oswald's chubby hand and led the way. Katharine and Freddie followed, with Father prodding them from behind.

Mother had left her handkerchief to mark the secret

door. "It's Lottie who discovered this. We have to give the lowest board a hard bang." She banged several times, with no help from Katharine and Freddie. At last the door swung open.

Father held the door and looked in. The window was open, and the bright July evening light revealed every corner. "A secret room!" he exclaimed. "How extraordinary." Then he saw his clock. "What's that doing here? That's my father's clock."

When Father had seen everything else in the secret room, he still remained most disturbed by his clock. "I've missed it. A clock of one's father's cannot be replaced. How could you steal it from me? My own children," he said when he had come out of the secret room.

He turned to Mother. "I don't see how all this went unnoticed. I thought Miss Pritt kept such a watchful eye on them. Well?" he asked, frowning down at Katharine and Freddie. He seemed very tall.

Freddie shrugged; then Katharine shrugged. She was going to do exactly what Freddie did.

"We got a moment here, a moment there," said Freddie vaguely.

"I don't know *how* we did it," Katharine replied. "I found Alice at the park."

"Who's Alice?" roared Father.

"The frog," whispered Katharine.

Fortunately Father had his mind on the Pospinwalls. He sent Mother down to dress. She had to drag Oswald away, for he loved the "fithies" in the crystal punch bowl.

Then Father spoke very gravely to Katharine and Freddie about how it is wrong to lie and steal. "You are too old to spank," he said, "but you will be punished severely. Your mother and I must talk. Your first punishment is this: empty this room now. It is no longer yours. Return all the stolen goods—everything. Free the animals in the garden and get that mouse out of the house. Our effort has been to get rid of mice, not to invite them in. Then come and report to me, because I have to check. I can't trust you anymore."

He took his beloved clock in his arms and started down the attic stairs. Halfway down, he stopped and looked up at them strangely. "It's quite something," he said. "A lot of work has gone into your secret room. Handmade shelves, eh? You've been alone a lot, children, haven't you?" He gave them a queer look before hurrying downstairs.

It was surprising how quickly the secret room was emptied, considering how long it had taken to fill it. In no time everything was back in its proper place. Eloise looked curiously at the dirty dishes and silverware in the sink. The day maids would probably have tantrums over the pile of dirty towels taken from the suitcase in the attic, which Katharine left on the pantry floor.

She and Freddie carried the punch bowl down to the garden and poured Sir and Madam back into the stone pool.

Freddie dropped Jack in the grass. As soon as the little mouse was freed, he disappeared under the foundation of the house.

"Hurrah! We'll see him again!" cried Freddie.

Katharine decided stubbornly not to free Alice in the garden. She left her, in her box, in the toolshed. She would take her back to the pond in Central Park tomorrow.

Bit by bit the room was stripped. Katharine and Freddie moved the shelves, now empty, against the secret door to keep it open. Then they rolled up the Oriental rug and brought it down to the library.

They went back to the attic to see if they had forgotten anything. Nothing was left in the secret room except the curtains, the table, and the shelves, propped against the door. The room looked desolate. A few dark chocolate crumbs on the floor reminded Katharine of their last, happy night there.

"Should we close the door?" asked Katharine.

"Why bother?" said Freddie.

It was just another room now. Katharine thought that Mother would probably use it as a closet. "Freddie, how do you think Father will punish us?" she asked. "Is he going to take Arthur away?"

When they got to the fourth floor, Lottie came out of her room dressed in her day-off clothes and carrying a suitcase. "I'm so glad to see you," she exclaimed. "I wouldn't leave without saying good-bye." She gave them each a peppermint stick. "I'll miss you, handsome—and you, too, Miss Katharine."

"Why do you have your suitcase?" asked Katharine.

"Oh, you'll find out. Ask your mother and father. I don't know how pleased they are about it, but I am."

She blushed crimson. "Good-bye, sweethearts." Lottie disappeared down the stairs.

Katharine and Freddie ran down to Father's and Mother's rooms, but they stopped short at the entrance to Mother's dressing room. Mother was sitting at her dressing table, and Father was standing over her. They were shouting at each other. Katharine had never heard them fight before.

"Lottie's leaving has nothing to do with me!" cried Mother. "She's given notice simply because Gifford has, that's all. They're planning to be married."

"That's not all," shouted Father. "It's unbelievable. Your maid, your chauffeur, and your nurse leave in one afternoon, and we discover that your children have been having a secret life in the attic. What kind of household have you been running?"

Mother didn't seem able to answer that. "Children, what do you want?" she asked Katharine and Freddie.

"Father, we've put all the things back," said Freddie timidly.

"Lottie is leaving?" asked Katharine, fingering her peppermint stick nervously in her pocket.

"She's getting married," said Mother. She held out her arms to Katharine and Freddie, and they came to her. "It's very romantic. Gifford and Lottie fell in love in our house."

"Really, Diana. When will you grow up?" said Father. "Everything's a childish game to you. You cannot be relied upon! Now there's no one to take care of the children, and I must go to see the Pospinwalls alone.

And explain why their nurse has left us." He stormed out, slamming the door.

"Oh, he's right, absolutely right," said Mother. "I'm a failure." She laid her head in her arms on the dressing table and sobbed. "It's my fault Miss Pritt left," she said between sobs. "I never could get used to having a nurse. I liked taking care of you myself, and she must have felt that."

What had Mother said? Katharine listened very carefully.

"Oh, you might as well know," said Mother, sitting up. "All those conferences I had with Miss Pritt were because I wanted to be with you more than she would allow. I tried to soften her rules. We were fighting over you."

Katharine could not believe her ears. All this time she had thought Mother had stopped loving them. "Don't cry, Mother," she said. She gave her a hankie from the dresser.

Freddie patted Mother's back, but this kindness only made her cry harder. "I know why you had your secret room," she said. "You were trying to escape our new life. And I was too busy to help you."

Mother sat up very straight and dried her eyes. "I know you hated Miss Pritt," she said, as if admitting it for the first time. "Well, I don't care how excellent all New York thinks she is. I'm glad she's gone. She wasn't the right nurse for our household." Mother blew her nose. "Please forgive me, children. I had never hired a nurse before and didn't know what to expect.

Father was so pleased with Miss Pritt. I should have stood up to him."

"It's all right, Mother," said Katharine, afraid Mother would start weeping again.

Now that Mother had stopped crying, they heard crying coming from the closet. It was Oswald. He had been playing with Mother's shoes. Mother's crying must have started him off. Freddie picked him up and put him in Mother's lap. Then he dared to ask whether he could go down to the storage room to see how Arthur was.

"Oh, bring him to the nursery," said Mother. "What difference does it make now? He's only a puppy. It would be too cruel to punish him by leaving him alone." Mother sighed. "I just hope Father gets into the law firm. Things are so bad, they can't get worse."

But they did. Katharine knew the moment supper was over and Father walked into the nursery. His hands were in his pockets and his shoulders were slumped.

"You were missed, Diana," he said. "Especially by Jack Pospinwall. I said you had a headache. It's awkward about Miss Pritt. I didn't tell them she quit."

"What about the firm?" exclaimed Mother.

Father looked down at his shoes. "They don't want me," he said. "Oh, they put it nicely. There isn't enough work in the firm right now." He stood, staring at his shoes.

Mother jumped up from the nursery chair. "Oh, that is terrible! How could they refuse you?" She put her arms around him. "My darling, I'm so sorry. It's awful that you had to hear such bad news by yourself."

Suddenly Arthur dashed out from under the nursery table. Katharine and Freddie pounced on him and made him sit in a corner. Arthur was very unwilling to sit. So they sat on the floor beside him and held him. This was no time for Father to be bothered by Arthur!

Father and Mother huddled together on the nursery chairs and talked. Father kept exclaiming, "I had my heart set on it!" and Mother said, "I should have done more for you."

Oswald had fallen asleep on the floor by his building blocks. Father and Mother didn't even bother to carry him to bed. Katharine was amazed. She hadn't realized Father cared this much about the law firm. She hadn't known Mother cared. They weren't even talking about the secret room and their children being thieves!

"Father's so disappointed he doesn't even notice Arthur," whispered Freddie. "I don't think he knows Arthur exists." Freddie gave Arthur his shoe to chew on, but Arthur growled at it.

"Hush!"

Freddie fed Arthur some leftover meat from supper. It was a job keeping him quiet.

Katharine was thinking hard. "Freddie," she whispered. "I'm beginning to see why Mother had a nurse for us. Mother loves to take care of us herself, but she can't do it all the time. She has to help Father with—"

"Katharine!" interrupted Freddie. "Stop chatting away and help!" He was stretched out on the floor, hanging on to Arthur's hind legs, and Arthur was about to wiggle free.

Katharine picked Arthur up and held him in her lap. She petted him and, much to her surprise, he rested his chin on her leg and fell asleep. It was never easy to talk to Freddie about loving Mother and Father, Katharine thought, but she promised herself that if they ever had another nurse, she would get along with her. At least she would try.

Father and Mother were still talking. Suddenly Katharine said to them, "Father's the *best* lawyer in the world and the smartest. The Pospinwalls are going to be sorry!"

Mother smiled. "Katharine's right," she said. Katharine must have cheered her up, because Mother patted Father's hand and said, "We have so many friends. Some other opportunity will come your way. We'll find it together."

Father got up and paced around the room, his hands in his pockets. He stopped over Katharine. "What's that in your lap?" he asked.

"That's Arthur," she said, her heart leaping.

"Arthur?" asked Father. He was smiling. "Is he named after King Arthur?"

"Yes," said Freddie. "He's wellborn. He has a long pedigree. He's the most spirited pup in the litter!"

"He looks very well behaved," said Father, and turned back to talk with Mother again. He hadn't said a word about getting rid of Arthur.

That night Father came into Katharine's bedroom to read *King Arthur*. Katharine and Freddie snuggled on either side of him. He said, "Now don't think you have been excused for lying and stealing. Your mother and I will discuss a punishment and tell you tomorrow." He opened the book where his marker was, then gave Katharine and Freddie a queer look, the same look he had given them halfway down the attic stairs when he had remarked how much they had been alone. Now he said, "It's a disgrace that I haven't read these last chapters. I've been too wrapped up in myself."

Father kept them up very late while he finished the book. There was no Miss Pritt to scowl at her watch and complain that it was getting late. Katharine didn't understand the whole story, but she liked the deep sound of Father's voice, and she liked his strong arm around her. And there in her lap, asleep again and panting gently, was Arthur.

·20·

I T WAS RAINING. Katharine sat on the window seat in the nursery, chewing a pencil and thinking. Ten days had gone by since the secret room had been discovered. The day after, she had started writing in her diary again. Now she read over what she had written:

July 16. Our punishment is no bisicles. Father was going to buy us Spalding bisicles with hand brakes and rubber tires. Now I am longing for one.

July 19. Today I went to the Stimson School. I am acsepted. I met a nice girl, Winifred. She has red hair. She loves animals. She took me to the science room, and they have snakes and caterpillers in cages. School is over for the summer, but Winifred is making up work. Her chair tipped over. What a crash! Also she kept me out of the class extra long looking at the caterpillers. Mother thinks she is naughty. I like her.

Katharine put down her diary and smiled. Winifred was going to be in fourth class with her. School would

175

not be so bad. She turned to a fresh page in the diary and began to write. *July 25. I AM SO HAPPY WITHOUT MISS PRITT. Father took us to Coney Island yesterday. We went on all the rides.* She stopped writing and looked at Freddie, who was seated at the nursery table lost in an adventure story. She didn't want Freddie reading her diary. She would have to hide it.

She wrote, *I feel so sad about Father.* He had decided to start his own law firm, continuing in the office he already had. He needed more clients. Every evening he came home from work looking worn out, his shoulders slumped; he said it was hard to find new clients.

"Ahem!"

Katharine looked up from her diary. Mr. Sloat was standing in the nursery with his nose in the air. "Madam wishes you to come downstairs," he said. "A crate has arrived from Mr. Oswald Wolcott."

Katharine and Freddie raced out the door with Arthur, a black streak, at their heels.

Mother was in the front hall by a large wooden box. She handed Freddie a screwdriver. "Please, Mr. Carpenter, will you open this for us? I expect it's the portrait of me that Uncle Oswald promised."

It was. Mother stood the painting against the wall and looked fondly at it. It was a picture of a girl in a pretty lace gown. But the girl in the dress was not particularly pretty. She had a long, pale face, and her arms were skin and bones.

"Mother, is that really you?" asked Katharine.

"Yes," said Mother. "Let's get Freddie's opinion. Did I look like Katharine?"

"Yes," Freddie said, although he hardly looked at the painting. He was examining the crate. "Mother, can I use the wood from this crate to make something? It's not going to stop raining, and there's nothing to do."

"I'll help," said Katharine.

"I don't need help," said Freddie.

"How about the two of you building something for your secret room?" asked Mother. "Now that Father and I have given it back to you, you never go there."

Katharine looked at Freddie. They both shrugged. Ever since the secret room had been discovered, it had lost its charm. It just seemed like a very small room, out of the way in the attic.

"I know!" exclaimed Freddie. "I can make a dog-house for Arthur. Please, Mother!"

"What about Katharine helping?"

"All right," said Freddie. Sometimes he forgot the help she had been in the days of the secret room. Together they picked up the crate. But before leaving the hall, Katharine took a last look at the thin figure in the painting. She thought, Perhaps I will grow up to be pretty like Mother—but I still won't change my clothes and hats every hour, the way she does.

Soon Katharine and Freddie were up in the nursery, happily hammering and sawing. The old door with the vise was once again in the nursery, placed over two trunks, which were packed for Long Island.

Mother sat on the floor with Oswald, painting a picture. Everyone was surprised when Father appeared in the nursery, home early from work.

"Darling! Is everything all right?" asked Mother.

"Er, Diana, there's someone here to see you—the nurse you interviewed from the agency," he said. "She says you told her to come today. It's Miss Stoner."

Father moved out of the doorway, and Katharine saw a big, plain woman. She had a crooked mouth and a nose that swooped to one side.

Mother sprang to her feet and exclaimed, "Gracious! Is it already July twenty-fifth? I'm so sorry. I confess I forgot about your coming today. I haven't even told the children yet. I apologize to everyone."

Miss Stoner was staring down at Mother, her eyes popping out. Mother could not offer her hand, for it had green and yellow paint on it.

A nurse! Mother had hired one after all. In spite of all Katharine's promises to herself, tears came to her eyes. She turned away, so no one could see. She picked up Arthur and buried her face in his black ruff.

"Please excuse our appearance," said Mother, blushing. Father was embarrassed, too, pulling at his whiskers as he had done the day Miss Pritt arrived and found them in a mess of clay and sawdust. Katharine became aware that the floor around her and Freddie was strewn with wood chips and nails and boards. She looked nervously at Miss Stoner. She remembered Miss Pritt saying she would soon have the place in order, and the children, too.

Mother said, "Come here, children, and meet Miss Stoner." Katharine came forward and did her best curtsy. She was determined to get on with this nurse, if it was possible.

Mother sneezed and covered her nose with her hand.

"Dear, your nose is green," said Father, smiling.

"Oh, my goodness," said Mother.

Katharine smiled, too, and dried her eyes.

Father kept on smiling his most handsome smile at everyone. "Miss Stoner has arrived in the nick of time," he said. "Even though we're going to Long Island at the end of the week, I may be called back to the city on business. I have not been happy about the idea of leaving you, Diana, alone with this brood of children and their wild dog." He winked at Katharine and Freddie. Then he took a card from his pocket and gave it to Mother. "I just received this invitation to dinner tonight from my . . . new client," he said. "He is none other than Mr. Bowles. He came to my office today and asked me to be his lawyer on a very important case."

"What good news!" exclaimed Mother. "Children, you must remember Mr. Bowles—at least you must remember his socks." She laughed merrily. "He is very important in the insurance business. Others will follow him. This will lead to many new clients!"

Father nodded. Katharine noticed that he was standing straight and tall and looked like his old self.

"Indeed we will go to the dinner," said Mother. She turned to Miss Stoner. "I'm sorry not to have prepared for your coming today. We're happy to see you. I'll help you get settled later. Now I had better do something about my hair and my green nose if I am going out to dinner. I'll be back a little later. Meanwhile, you can get acquainted with the children. Katharine, please show Miss Stoner her room." Mother blew a kiss and followed Father down the hall.

It was quiet in the nursery. Katharine, Freddie, and Oswald looked up at the tall Miss Stoner. Behind her, Katharine saw the rain pouring against the window-panes. She felt numb inside.

Woof! Woof! Arthur had decided, a little late, to be a watchdog and bark at Miss Stoner. He jumped on her skirts and, when she leaned down to him, he grabbed a corner of the scarf at her neck and pulled it off. He ran around the nursery with the scarf in his teeth.

"Stop it, Arthur!" yelled Katharine.

"Come here!" yelled Freddie.

Miss Stoner chased Arthur, but he kept escaping her. They were making circles around the nursery table. Arthur was playing, wagging his tail. At last Miss Stoner knelt down, caught him, and held him in her lap. "He's a lively one," she said.

"He was the most spirited pup in the litter," said Katharine proudly.

Miss Stoner took back her scarf, placed it on top of Arthur's head, and tied it under his chin. "There!" she said, and burst into laughter. Her whole big body shook, she was laughing so hard. She suddenly seemed very young.

Now everyone was laughing, even Oswald, who said, "Silly doggy."

Miss Stoner untied her scarf, put Arthur down, and stood up. Then Katharine said politely, "Come this way, Miss Stoner. I'll show you your room."

"Oh, you may call me Aurelia," said the tall young woman.

Katharine was too surprised to answer. But Freddie said, "I don't like being called Frederick. My name is Freddie."

"All right, Freddie," said Aurelia.

Freddie gave Katharine a satisfied nod as she led Aurelia to Miss Pritt's old room. Aurelia was very pleased with it. "Your mother is such a nice lady," she said. "My mother never played with us. Of course she didn't have the time—we're twelve children." Then a worried look crossed her face. She bent down to Katharine and whispered, "I've never been a nurse before. I'm a bit nervous, to tell the truth."

"Oh, it's easy," said Katharine. "I know all about it. The nurse we had before you had a lot of experience. She had been a nurse for thirty-one years. Oswald's a bit spoiled, but I can help you with him. I'll help you!" she exclaimed, feeling suddenly very excited and happy. She looked up at Miss Stoner—Aurelia—and smiled.

NIKI YEKTAI holds a master's degree in education from New York University and lives in New York City with her husband, an artist, and their three children. She has also written *Hi Bears, Bye Bears*, illustrated by Diane deGroat, an IRA Children's Choice. This is her first novel.